The Lady's Sinful Secret

BOOK 4: THE SINS & SCANDALS SERIES

KELLY BOYCE

The Sins & Scandals Series

While there are those who spend their time in modest pursuits, upholding propriety befitting the lords and ladies of the ton, it would seem that for others, scandal is just a sin away...

AN INVITATION TO SCANDAL
A SCANDALOUS PASSION
A SINFUL TEMPTATION
THE LADY'S SINFUL SECRET
SURRENDER TO SCANDAL
A SINNER NO MORE
THE SWEETEST SIN
A MOST SCANDALOUS CHRISTMAS
A HINT OF SCANDAL

For John – because every girl needs a white knight.

Chapter One

The sweeping landscape, filled with rolling hills and hardy wildflowers, stretched out to meet the early October sky. Gloria shivered against the unexpected chill of the morning as it infiltrated the wool of her plum riding habit. Shifting in her saddle, she took in the beauty displayed along the outer edges of Sheridan Park where an invisible line separated Blackbourne land from that belonging to the Sutherlands.

All around her, the tips of the leaves had started to change their colors, turning from a lush green to the promised bounty of rich reds, oranges and yellows. The beauty was a sight to behold and the fresh air and invigorating ride a welcome diversion from the commotion in her home as her children busied themselves with preparations for a party celebrating her upcoming birthday.

Not that she didn't appreciate their desire to throw a party in her honor, but try as she might, she could not seem to muster the same level of enthusiasm for the upcoming event. What was there to celebrate after all? Getting older? Being alone? Lacking purpose? Her husband was dead and buried, bringing an end to a rather insufferable marriage and now, as she stood on the precipice of turning nine and forty, she realized her work as a wife and parent was...done.

Over.

"Perhaps you should take a lover to distract yourself."

Her dear friend, Lorena, had made the bold suggestion. Imagine such a thing! The very idea left her scandalized. The Dowager Countess of Blackbourne did not take lovers. She...she...

Gloria let out a sharp breath. In truth, she didn't know what a dowager countess did once her children were grown and married, but likely riding about in the early morning until your cheeks flushed and your nose turned red was a much safer bet than taking a lover. Her family had suffered enough scandal over the years without her adding more to it.

Besides, she'd had a lover once, a long time ago, and the results had been disastrous. Not the type of distraction she cared to repeat.

A sound disrupted her thoughts. She pulled on the reins of her mount and turned in her saddle. In the distance near a copse of trees, a young boy stood looking up the thick trunk of an old oak. He called out to something above him, but the breeze whipped his words away from her ears.

Curious, Gloria nudged her mare and slowly approached. She did not recognize him. Strange. She prided herself on knowing all of the Blackbourne tenants and their families. As she drew nearer, she took note of the boy's clothing. Well-tailored and expensive, he appeared more a gentleman farmer in miniature than one of the stable boys or caretakers.

Odd.

"C'mon now, Shadow. I promise ya a nice shiny bauble if you'll come on down." The boy rested his chest against the tree and wrapped thin arms around its massive trunk.

Gloria noted the tinge of a brogue dancing around his

words and a tingle of familiarity made the hair at the nape of her neck prickle.

"Have you lost something up the tree?"

The boy whirled about, his feet slipping out from under him on the dewy grass. He landed on the damp earth with a thud and a wince before scrambling back up and executing a hasty bow.

"Forgive me, my lady. I didn't mean to disturb ya."

She smiled and tilted her head to one side. Something about the boy seemed oddly familiar, yet she could not place it. He had a sweet face; almost elfish in a way, with blond hair and pale blue eyes softening his sharp features.

"I'm not disturbed at all, though I do find myself quite curious. Might I ask your name, sir?"

"Callum Sutherland, my lady." He gifted her with another courtly bow.

The name rang through her heart and rattled her composure. She pulled her shoulders back and forced her smile to remain in place. It meant nothing. In all likelihood, the Sutherlands had scores of children. There was no reason to believe that—

She shook the thought off before it could take hold. She had avoided the Sutherlands for over thirty years. She would not allow a single encounter with one of their offspring to cause her concern or worry now.

"I see. And are you visiting the estate?" The Sutherland lands abutted a small portion of Sheridan Park. Likely the boy had followed the pathway that cut through the trees just off in the distance.

"No, my lady. We've come to live here now that my uncle has passed on."

Gloria swallowed, but it did not release the lump that lodged swiftly in her throat.

"Your uncle?" Dismay rippled through her belly and

threaded up toward her heart, the reason for the boy's familiarity becoming clear. She touched the silver locket at her breast.

"Uncle Donald. I only met 'im but one time. He passed a few months ago."

"I see." Her mare shifted beneath her and she loosened her hold on the reins, realizing it had tightened the moment the boy said his name.

"I'm sorry if I was trespassin'. Shadow isn't quite familiar with 'is surroundin's as yet. He flew off and won't come down if I don't give 'im something shiny."

Gloria glanced up to where the boy pointed. A large black crow rested on a thick branch. As if aware it had become the subject of speculation, it let out a loud caw and ruffled its shiny feathers. Its black eyes fixed directly on her as if it sensed her secrets and would reveal them if she did not act quickly.

Ridiculous. Obviously the crow knew no such things and was hardly in a position to reveal anything, given its inability to communicate beyond a caw. Yet guilt filtered through her as it continued to stare. She wound the reins around the pommel of her saddle and reached for the emerald and gold ring fitted securely on her finger over her riding glove. She slid it off and handed it down to the boy. He gave her a dubious look.

Gloria waved her hand. "Take it. It should do the trick if he likes shiny baubles."

"I can't take your jewels, my lady. Shadow likes to keep 'em."

"It is of no matter." Her late husband had showered her in jewels—not out of a sense of love, but to ensure she outshone all the other ladies and presented the image he wished to project to his peers. The baubles meant nothing to her. She would be well rid of them now. Well rid of the memories attached to them. "Take it."

With reluctance, Callum reached for the ring and then

backed up toward the tree. He made a clucking sound with his tongue, as she would have when calling to her favorite mare, and presented the trinket in the palm of his hand.

"Well c'mon then. This is what you wanted." He waved his hand and the sun glinted off the gold, catching the crow's attention. The bird called to him quietly, the sound reminding her of a cat's purr, then scuttled down the branch, craning its neck for a better look. After a bit of deliberation and coaxing from the boy, the crow hopped a little closer, then spread its wings to land on Callum's arm. "There. Now was that such a 'ard thing ta do, you silly bird?"

The crow purred in response. Such strange noises to hear from a species known for its sharp caw.

"Is he a pet?"

Callum shrugged. "I s'pose. Much as an animal with wings can be. He took a shine ta me a little bit ago. Da said he might someday go on 'is way, but so far he seems content ta stay put."

She smiled and nodded, then asked the question she had been dreading. "And your father, who is he?"

"Callum!"

The deep voice rang through the still morning air before the boy could answer, but it mattered little. Gloria would have recognized him regardless of the number of years that lay between now and the last time he'd spoken to her.

She turned and the man who had haunted her dreams and her memories for three decades stopped in his tracks.

"Glory…"

The name washed over her like a comforting balm soothing the wounds and scars time had left. In that moment, she was sixteen again, seeing him for the first time as he had come down over the hill, his trusty yellow hunting dog trotting along at his side. His lean build and broad shoulders gave way to a confidant gait and only the morning breeze had dared ruffle his dark hair. He'd smiled when he laid eyes upon her then, but he was not smiling now.

No, definitely not smiling. Any hint of laughter that lived in her memory was just that—a memory. In its place was the stern countenance of a man who brooked no disobedience or argument. His gaze glanced over her and the set of his jaw tightened.

Gloria refused to mimic his expression. Why should she? She had nothing to be angry with him for. She had put away her disappointment in that regard long ago. The destiny they had carved out when still barely more than children had been a fool's dream. She'd accepted that and the consequences that had come from it.

"Good morning, Arran." Arran. How long had it been since she'd said his name aloud? Heard him say hers, the one he had chosen for her? *Glory*. She sighed, unaware until that moment of how much she had needed to hear it. "I—I was not aware you had returned home."

He had yet to come closer. "I was not aware I was required to send you notice of my arrival, *Countess*."

The coldness in his tone lashed out and she swiftly inhaled, clutching her locket, a talisman against his harsh words. Unexpected tears glazed her eyes, but she blinked them back and continued to hold her forced smile in place. Her years with Blackbourne had taught her well.

"Indeed, I'm certain such was not required at all. Have you been home long?" She was vaguely aware of Callum coming to stand by her side. Of the strange purring that came from the crow balanced on his arm; the way its beak poked at the bauble the boy held in his hand. Little things. They were easier to focus on than the handsome man glowering at her from not twenty feet away.

"We arrived in August, shortly after Donald's passing."

"Yes, Callum only just informed me—" She released the

locket and motioned toward the boy. Arran's words sank in with deeper meaning, but before she could fully grasp what he meant, the bird hopped from Callum's arm to her hand. "Oh!"

It cawed quietly at her. How large it appeared up close, and yet weighed much less than one would expect. Its black eyes stared up at her, blinking, though she could detect no emotion within their depth. Much like the man standing before her, though once upon a time she could have read him like her favorite book, reciting the words without ever looking at the page. The crow moved its head and the tip of its beak lightly pecked the silver heart at her breast.

"Forgive me, m'lady." Callum gave a sheepish grin, lopsided with a hint of mischief and again the strange sensation passed through her that she looked at someone she already knew. "I believe 'e likes you."

Before she could answer, the boy made a clucking noise and the bird turned, its clawed feet pricking her skin through her leather gloves as it took flight to land on Callum's arm. If only her own escape would come so easily.

She had ridden from the stables in the hopes of discovering what she was to do with her future, instead she had stumbled into an upside down world where everything past had become present once more, without warning. One would think she'd have been given notice. A hint, at least, that everything she had stored away had sprung free from its hiding place and spilled out around her.

"I think his affection is for the shiny baubles more so than it is for me." Her voice shook despite her efforts to keep it steady.

Slowly—as her mind could not work at its usually swift pace under such circumstances—she recalled what Callum had told her only moments ago. *Had only moments passed?* He had come to live here upon his uncle's passing. As had Arran.

She turned and looked at the boy with new eyes. Of course. The sense of familiarity she'd felt found a home. She turned back to Arran.

"Callum is your son, then?" The corners of her mouth ached from holding her smile in place.

Arran inclined his head. The only acknowledgement she would receive. When had the deep blue of his eyes become so cold? Had they always been like that and she'd simply been too young and in love to see it? Or was it a more recent development? And if he had a son, then it stood to reason he also had a—

She swallowed. "And Mrs. Sutherland?"

His hard gaze left her and rested on his son. He gestured toward her. "Callum, may I present the great lady of Sheridan Park, the Countess of Blackbourne."

If the boy noted the undercurrent between them, he gave no outward appearance beyond a curious glint in his sharp gaze. Instead, keeping the crow balanced skillfully on his arm, he executed his third courtly bow of the morning.

"It's ma' great pleasure to make your acquaintance, m'lady."

"The feeling is quite mutual. Although..." She looked at Arran. "I am the Dowager Countess, now. Nicholas has married and bears the title Earl of Blackbourne. His wife, Abigail, is the new Countess." *He's dead,* she wanted to shout. *I'm free!* But she didn't. It hardly mattered now. He had married another. Moved on. Arran gave no hint he cared one way or the other over her marital state. Her heart tore open and she clamped her jaw tightly against the pain.

"Then it appears you have everything you ever wanted." He glanced in the direction of Sheridan House. "My compliments."

His words hurt, far more than she'd thought possible after all this time. Did he still blame her for choosing Blackbourne?

Did he not understand she would never have turned away from him without good reason? Or had hurt dissolved any sense in this regard?

She took a deep breath and resurrected the regal bearing years of breeding and comportment classes had drilled into her. "Do I? I was not aware. Thank you for informing me. I shall ensure I keep that in mind going forward."

His mouth pulled into a tight line, the only indication he understood the sarcasm laced through her words. "And I will ensure Callum understands where the boundaries of our properties are, so he does not cross them again."

"Callum is welcome on Sheridan land any time." She looked at the boy, her smile easy when she did so. "There are great places to explore and many adventures to be had."

But before his son could answer, Arran spoke again. "If you will excuse us, my lady. We are expected elsewhere."

A dismissal. Cold and succinct, the hint of his Scottish brogue rolling around it, stronger now than what she remembered. Had he returned to his birthplace following the war? Is that where he'd met his wife? Where Callum had been born and raised until the death of his uncle brought them both home? There were so many questions she wanted to ask, so many years to fill in, but his brusque manner made it clear he did not care to keep her informed. He did not care to have anything to do with her at all.

"My apologies, Mr. Sutherland. It was not my intention to keep you."

Except it had been, once upon a time. She had promised him her heart, bound their souls together and vowed it would be forever. How naïve they had been. How blindly optimistic that the world would give its blessing and open its arms to welcome them.

"Perhaps I will see you at the Assembly this evening?" How she loathed the hope that echoed in her voice.

"You will not, my lady." The terseness of his tone cut her to the quick. Sharp and without compromise. He gave a curt bow. It possessed none of the flourish of his son's. "Good day."

She nodded, the only response she could manage at his outright dismissal of her. As she watched his retreating back, she noted the fatherly hand he rested on Callum's shoulder. Something her son, Nicholas, had never received from the man who had raised him.

Again the questions and doubt came back to roost.

Had she done the right thing?

Chapter Two

Upon returning to Havelock Manor, Arran retreated to his study and closed the door behind him, swiftly crossing the familiar hardwood with its worn carpet and creaking floorboards to reach the supply of brandy his brother had left behind. He poured a glass and downed it in one gulp, wishing for all he was worth that it packed the same punch as the whiskey he'd grown accustomed to in Dumfries.

Home.

The word meant little to him. He'd discovered long ago home was not a place. Not a spot one could pinpoint on a map. Home was a person. And his home, the one that had lived in his heart, the one he had built the dreams of his future upon, had been destroyed beyond repair.

For years, he had avoided returning to Sutherland Estates, avoided belonging anywhere or to anyone. His heart had proven it could not be trusted and as such, he had taken it out of commission. But eventually, the wandering life of a soldier wore thin and the need to set down roots brought him to Dumfries and to Jean. Guilt he'd burrowed deep in his heart, flared. He had not loved her. Did not dare to. She had deserved better. It wasn't until Callum had been born, and he was introduced to a different kind of love, that he'd stopped looking to the horizon, stopped wishing for a love he'd once had and lost.

Instead, he'd turned his attention to his son, determined Callum would never doubt his father's steadfast affections. Never worry that there were others who held greater importance. Never feel like an afterthought, the way his own father had made him feel. As *she* had made him feel.

He ground his back teeth until they hurt. He had not expected such a violent reaction to seeing her again. A reaction compounded when he saw the locket he'd given her, hanging from its silver chain, the heart at its end nestled against her breast.

Why had she kept it?

He shook his head. It mattered not.

He'd spent the past two months avoiding any contact with the Sheridans. He'd forbidden his sister or her offspring to comment on any of them while in his presence. He wanted nothing to do with the clan created by a man who was instrumental in destroying the life he'd wanted. And he wanted even less to do with the woman who had forsaken her promises to him in order to join them.

The pain should have lessened over the years, blunted by the passing of time. He'd learned today how wrong such an assumption had been.

She was breathtaking. Even more so than the first time he'd seen her. The years had been more than kind. If anything, they had softened where they should have and defined where they needed to. And her eyes—those damnable silver eyes— even from the distance that had separated them he could see they had not dimmed in the least and the thick blonde hair, though coifed and controlled, still curled softly along the arch of her cheekbone. How well he remembered its silky texture drifting between his fingers.

He poured another glass and downed it as quickly as the first. How many did he need to dull the burning in his chest, the sense that he had fallen down a rabbit hole and landed in a life he no longer recognized as his own?

He'd been rude to her. Beyond rude, really. Positively surly. He did not regret it.

He regretted it a little.

Another drink, yet the numbness continued to evade him. "Bugger, hell and damn!"

He shoved the glass away and let it skid across the smooth mahogany surface of the bar. The same bar where his father had given him his first taste of whiskey. He'd been all of nine years old and his mother had just died. A grief he and Callum shared in common, though Arran had not given his son the same remedy his father had him. He shook the memory off. One painful remembrance at a time was enough.

He stalked to the window and glared out at the bucolic setting. He'd been a fool to think he could avoid the meeting forever. He'd been aware of Blackbourne's death. His sister, Beatris, had informed him practically the moment he'd arrived back at Havelock, thinking he'd want to know. It was then he'd decreed the subject off limits.

That part of his life had ended when Glory refused to respond to his letters. Pathetic letters where he'd begged her to leave Blackbourne and run away with him. Letters that came back; return to sender. As if he'd ceased to exist. As if what they had shared no longer mattered.

Had it ever mattered? Or had he been nothing more than a diversion? A plaything.

God, what a fool he'd been! Even worse though, was that piece of him he could not root out. The piece that took one glance at her and wished to have her still. To hold her in his arms and feel her skin against his.

He closed his eyes and leaned his forehead against the cool glass pane. He despised her. And he loved her. A truth he could not deny. A torment he could not escape.

He should never have returned.

"There you are. I have been looking all over for you."

Arran opened his eyes and turned. Beatris stood in the doorway of his study, her hands folded across her belly.

Until his return to Havelock Manor, it had been half a decade since he'd seen his sister. Older than he by a handful of years, she'd turned pleasantly plump and seemed happy with her husband, and their two grown children, though, according to their regular correspondence, rather dismayed that neither her son nor daughter had yet to marry.

Correspondence had seemed preferable to visits, though Beatris had been to see him on a few occasions. A favor he had not returned. He had hoped distance and a new life would erase the pain of his past.

It had not.

"Good morning, sister dear. You're up earlier than usual." His sister kept what he referred to as *London hours*. He, on the other hand, preferred to rise early and greet the day. There was much work to be done, as the estate had lain fallow during the last year of Donald's illness, despite his niece Judith's best attempts to manage things while tending to her father.

"I have had little choice. The Assembly is this evening, if you'll recall."

He did; he simply cared little for the social goings-on of his neighbors. Such gatherings were rife with the possibility of running into his past. Once was enough for one day.

"Patience is excited, I assume?" Beatris's daughter, despite a disastrous first Season, had thrown herself into each entertainment offered with such fervor it was a sight to behold. It was as if the events that had led Beatris to pack her daughter up and hide out in the country had never occurred. Hopefully Judith, being several years older than Patience, would have a tempering effect on his youngest niece's behavior.

"She is, though Patience has expressed a wish that you join us this time. Your presence would go a long way toward improving her standing amongst the townsfolk."

"She is the daughter of a baron with a rather sizeable dowry. I hardly think she needs her disagreeable uncle to assist her in meeting proper gentlemen. You and Judith will suffice."

Beatris smiled and took a breath. He knew what was coming and considered departing before she started, but his sister had tactically blocked the doorway.

"You cannot avoid them forever." *Them.* Meaning *her.*

"I am not attempting to avoid anyone."

She lifted one eyebrow. "You are an abominable liar, Arran Sutherland."

"That's Sir Arran to you," he teased, hoping to divert the conversation. His scheme failed.

"One would think a man with a knighthood would be braver, and not hide out in his castle to avoid running into a lady he once held an affection for, three decades previous."

"I live in a manor, not a castle. And I have already run into the lady in question." The admission left a sour taste on his tongue.

Beatris's warm brown eyes widened. "You have? When?"

Arran cleared his throat and did his best to affect a nonchalant air, as if the encounter had had little effect on him. "Just this morning. Callum was chasing Shadow and found himself on Sheridan Park lands."

"Well." Beatris worried her hands and nodded toward the bar where the decanter of brandy and his empty glass rested. "I suppose that explains why you've chosen to imbibe so early in the day."

He scowled at his sister's powers of observation. Did the woman miss nothing? "I happened to be thirsty. Do not read so much into it."

"Hmph. If there is nothing to read into it, then you will not mind accompanying us to the Assembly tonight."

"I am afraid I would mind very much. There is much work to be done and I do not have time for such frivolity."

"Arran, I know she hurt you, but it has been thirty years and you have been widowed for over two—"

He held up a hand, cutting off his sister's well-meant cajoling that he return to society. "I appreciate your concern, but I assure you, my lack of interest in social goings-on is based solely on my desire to put my energies into running the estate so that when I pass on, Callum will have something of worth to call his own. My reticence has nothing to do with pining for lost loves."

"Arran—"

Again he stopped her. "And if that is all, I need to attend to just such matters. I am certain you and the girls will enjoy yourselves without my presence. I never was much of a dancer anyway."

A bigail paced the receiving room in a pique while Gloria waved a rattle in front of her grandson's reaching hands. The boy, lovingly named Roddy, grew more cherubic by the day.

"I find it rather suspect that each time I have paid a visit they have not been in. Where is it that they are going? I have asked around and while Baroness Elmsley is well thought of, I cannot imagine she spends every day traipsing about the village paying calls. At some point, people would be returning the calls she has made, forcing her to stay at home to receive them."

Though Gloria had mentioned in passing to Marcus that she had met the new owner, she had refrained from telling anyone else. Her new son-in-law was not one to pry and she gave only a brief mention of the event as he had come upon her when she returned to the stables. Marcus was far too perceptive not to notice something was amiss. She shrugged it off as best she could, and did not speak of it further to the others. There was little point. Neither her son, daughter, or daughter-in-law knew of her past with the Sutherlands. A past that would easily explain the Sutherlands' reserve in welcoming a Sheridan into their home. It was a slight, to be certain, but not one undeserved. Still, she supposed some explanation was necessary to prevent further prying from her curious and determined daughter-in-law.

"I am afraid Blackbourne and Sir Douglas Sutherland had a rather discordant relationship." An understatement if ever one existed.

"But the late Lord Blackbourne is dead and buried, as is Sir Douglas. Surely they cannot hold Nicholas responsible for whatever acrimony existed between the two men!" She threw her arms up and flopped down onto the sofa next to Gloria. "Is there nothing you can do to smooth it over? Extend an olive branch of sorts? I would very much like to make their acquaintance and put matters back to rights. They are our neighbors, after all."

Neighbors. Indeed. That was how it had all started, was it not? The Sutherlands were landed gentry, their property gifted to them by the crown upon the elder Sutherland's knighting, an honor bestowed upon him for heroics in battle on behalf of the King. The south end of his property lay sandwiched between the land owned by her family and the countryseat of the Earl of Blackbourne. Her social-climbing parents had wanted little to do with the Sutherlands, convinced the Scots were beneath their station and did not deserve the one they held. Gloria had thought little of it until one day she came across Arran as he and his dog retrieved a wayward cow that had broken ranks and wandered off.

Then, the Sutherlands—one in particular—were all she could think of. And if she were honest with herself, she would admit there had not been a day since that she hadn't thought about the Sutherlands. One in particular. But thoughts and memories were all she had. Fate had torn them apart quite irrevocably. She had not expected to ever see him again.

Yet, here he was. Once again in her backyard. Perhaps fate was not done with them yet.

She tossed the idea aside and leaned down to kiss the downy hair on Roddy's head, black as night, just like his father's and his father's before him. Arran was married with a young son, much as she had been. There was no place in his life for her. That kind of thinking needed to stop this instant.

Easier said than done.

The brief glimpse she'd had of him refused to leave her. For years, she had wondered where he was, what he was doing, how he had fared. Was he as handsome as the man of her memories? Or had the years changed and altered him? As it turned out, time had strengthened and weathered him in ways that only served to enhance the sharp edges and angles of his lean form and broad shoulders. Thin lines fanned out from the outer edges of his deep blue eyes and a hint of gray peppered the temples of his inky black hair. He exuded a masculinity that made everything in her come alive, as if no time had passed at all.

"Gloria?"

"Hm? Oh, yes." Heat crept up her throat and bloomed in her cheeks. "I'm afraid I wouldn't be much help in repairing the discourse between our families, my dear. I fear my association to the late earl would only serve to rub salt into an old wound. But I applaud your willingness to want to bridge the divide."

Abigail leaned back against the cushions and reached over to absently touch her son's cheek, an unconscious show of affection. Abigail had taken to motherhood with great aplomb, despite her misgivings that she would fail miserably at it. Gloria could not have asked for a better mother for her grandchildren. Hopefully, now that Marcus and Rebecca had married, more would be in the offing not too far in the future. It gave her something to look forward to.

"Perhaps persistence is the key, then. I shall simply pay them visits until they have no choice but to be home to receive me, or risk the embarrassment of publically offending us. I'm sure they wouldn't want that."

"I would think not." Though the claim did not hold much conviction. If left to Arran, she had no doubt he would do just that and consider the insult well deserved, but perhaps his sister would have a change of heart. She had always rather liked Beatris, even if his sister had thought her and Arran a dangerous match.

Only further proof of the woman's sensible nature.

"Then I shall try again today and suggest to them I will sit on their doorstep until they return, if they find themselves not at home yet again."

Gloria smiled despite the trepidation that ran through her at the thought of mingling the two families once more.

No good could come of it.

Could it?

Chapter Three

"What else was I to do, Arran? We can hardly leave the Countess of Blackbourne standing on our front step awaiting our supposed return," Beatris said, her voice urgent and nervous as they hurried down the hallway toward the receiving room.

"I don't see why not, if that is what she was inclined to do." How he had become entangled in this matter escaped him. One moment he had been happily working away in his study and the next his sister had rushed in, all in a dither. "I suspect after a few moments she would have gone back to Sheridan Park, tired of waiting about."

Beatris scoffed. "Then you have not heard the stories about the new Countess. She is a bit of a bold one, if rumors are to be believed."

"I am not interested in rumors. Nor am I interested in meeting the new Countess."

"Well you've little choice. She is here now and she made an express wish to meet both of us. It would be the height of rudeness to deliver such a cut as to deny her request and could reflect badly on the girls."

After what the Sheridan family had done to him, rudeness seemed an appropriate response. But he did not care to explain that to his sister, nor admit how much his past association with the family affected him still.

"Fine. I will say my hellos and then be on my way. You and the girls can maintain the rest of the visit."

Beatris stopped outside the door to the receiving room and lowered her voice. "Judith has taken Patience out to meet the Maynards. And it will look unfavorably upon us if you do not stay long enough for a proper visit. I know you have no interest in society, but it is the world I live in, and given Patience's disastrous first Season and Judith's lack of proposals, slighting Lady Blackbourne will not help matters. Please, Arran!"

He pulled his mouth into a grim line. "Very well. For the girls. But let's make this a short visit, shall we?"

Beatris's palpable relief at his acquiescence did little to lift his spirits as they entered the room to face the new Countess of Blackbourne. As they said their hellos and Beatris made the proper introductions and apologized for not being home sooner to receive her calls, Arran studied the woman who had displaced Glory as Countess. She was a pretty little thing and while she did not embody the quiet, regal bearing of the previous Countess, she did possess a brilliant smile and energy that, despite his best intentions, he found quite engaging.

"I am so happy to finally make your acquaintance, Lady Elmsley, and sorry to have missed Miss Sutherland and Miss Elmsley, but I look forward to receiving all of you in the near future so we might become better acquainted."

Beatris gushed at the invitation and Arran had no doubt her nimble mind was already devising a plan whereby she could request the Countess's assistance in introducing Patience to any number of eligible bachelors bearing the Blackbourne stamp of approval. God save England from match-making mamas and their unmarried daughters.

"And, Sir Arran, how thrilled I am to meet you, though I am most sorry that it is under such sad circumstances. I did not have the good fortune of meeting your brother, but others speak most highly of him."

"That is kind of you to say."

Lady Blackbourne smiled at him and though his sister and the Countess continued their conversation, the latter's gaze continually drifted back to him, a curious expression on her pretty features. It was as if she were searching for something. Once the conversation turned to babies, he stood to leave and return to his office, but the Countess spoke before he could make his excuses. "Forgive me, Sir Arran, but I have the sense we have met before. Is such a thing possible?"

"It is highly unlikely, my lady. Unless you have traveled to Dumfries in the past decade."

"I think it is quite safe to say I have not. Still..." She shook her head and her smile became uncertain. "You bear a striking resemblance to—" She broke off whatever she had been about to say and let out a little laugh, but it rang hollow. The strange half-sentence hung in the air between them. He took a step forward as if he could somehow pluck its meaning out of thin air. But before he could decipher the comment, Lady Black-bourne waved her hand, brushing it away. "Well, that is neither here nor there, I suppose we all look like someone else to some degree, don't we? My reason for coming today is a simple one. I wish to personally invite you to a party."

Beatris sat up straighter and set her tea cup down. "A party?"

"Yes." Lady Blackbourne's smile widened, the uncertainty of a moment ago gone. "The Dowager Countess's birthday is approaching and we have decided a celebration is in order. It is in a fortnight and we do so hope you and your family can attend. I understand you are still in mourning over your brother, but—"

"Oh no," Beatris held out a hand. "I mean, yes. Of course, we miss Donald very much, but our brother was fond of parties and he instructed us before he passed that we were not to sit about brooding after he left. And truly," She glanced up at Arran with a firm gaze. "I believe a party would go a long way in helping Judith move forward from her father's death. The poor girl has not quite been herself since he fell ill."

Lady Blackbourne clapped her hands. "It is settled then. I am so pleased. Our families have had a rocky past, I understand, but those who created it are gone now and I would very much like to become the best of neighbors. Wouldn't you?"

The Countess's gaze left his sister and landed on him, pointed and direct, her meaning well taken. Unfortunately, she had been misinformed. The parties who had created that rocky past were *not* all dead and buried. Two of them were still very much alive. He had no intention of improving relations between them. Glory had made her choice. He would not grovel for her favor now, as he had back then.

The Dowager Countess of Blackbourne could celebrate her birthday without him.

Gloria glanced at her reflection in the mirror of her dressing table, leaning in to see the fine lines around her eyes, the first hint of grooves appearing around the corners of her mouth. Though the closer she came to the mirror, the more blurred the details became.

She sighed. She needed spectacles. Dear heaven, when had that happened?

A soft knock sounded at her bedchamber door and she

leaned back from the mirror, her reflection clearing as she did. "Come in."

Her son, Nicholas, opened the door, looking every inch a gentleman in his evening clothes, and yet somehow still maintaining a hint of the rogue he had always been. She turned and smiled up at him. If she had done nothing else right in her life, her children would remain her crowning achievement, a legacy to be proud of.

"You look beautiful, Mother."

"Do I?" She had never been one to fish for compliments. It bothered her that she felt the need to now, but seeing Arran again made the years that had passed all the more prominent. She stared into the reflective glass. She was not so foolish to think she hadn't retained some of her former beauty, as she fast approached her fiftieth year, but neither did she mislead herself into thinking that beauty would last forever.

"I dare say the younger ladies will be quite jealous when you steal their thunder."

"You are too much the gallant, my dear."

What had Arran thought when he looked at her? Did he see a faded image of the woman he used to know? Or did he even care? So much had happened, so many things she wished to explain. But had too much time passed? She feared the answer was yes, and the idea of that made her quite sad.

Gloria stood, the silk and satin of her gown rustling about her. "Is it time to go?"

"It is. Roddy is fast asleep and Abigail has deemed if we do not leave this instance, we shall be beyond fashionably late. Though, I think when I arrive at the Assembly with the two most beautiful ladies in England on either arm, I will be heartily forgiven."

"Will the others be attending?"

"Indeed. Rebecca has convinced Marcus it is his duty as a landowner to partake in such activities and despite his best arguments to the contrary, my little sister seems to have done the impossible and wrapped the poor man about her finger."

Gloria took Nicholas's proffered arm. "And Lord and Lady Huntsleigh?"

"They will be in attendance as well. Abigail has insisted Caelie has not increased to such a degree that she need hide away, and Spence never likes to miss a party."

"Wonderful. It will be lovely to have us all in the same place once again, if only for an evening." And in the event the Sutherlands attended, a buffer of loved ones around her would help to distract from the unsolicited emotions Arran stirred within her.

A n army of candles lit the Assembly's main room and the crush of bodies warmed the vast area, chasing away the autumn chill. Soon winter would arrive. Short, cold days buried beneath a white blanket of snow that would hang thick on the branches of every tree and reflect the sun's rays with such potency as to hurt the eyes just to gaze upon it.

Gloria had always loved winter at Sheridan Park. Mostly because her husband had preferred to remain in London to oversee his business interests through the day and, as she had discovered after his death, warm the bed of his long-time mistress through the night.

The irony of which had not been lost on her. He had accused her of infidelity, a charge she did not attempt to cry innocent of. She had loved a man not her husband. A man who *should* have been her husband if she'd had her way. But her wants and desires had been shoved aside in favor of her parents' social-climbing ways.

Her husband had lorded her affair over her for the entirety

of their marriage, using it to keep her in place, reminding her always of her weakness and disgraceful behavior for having broken the marriage vows she'd been forced to make. Perhaps he was right. Perhaps she had been weak and her actions reprehensible. But even so, all these years later, she did not regret them. Not once. Not for a moment.

It was that fact that had fuelled Blackbourne's loathing, she was certain. Yet, he'd done the same with no thought of repercussion.

Spencer Kingsley, the Earl of Huntsleigh appeared at her side. "Would you care to dance, my lady? I'm afraid my wife has decided she is too tired to partake at the moment and I find myself quite at a loss."

Gloria smiled, thankful for the distraction Huntsleigh created. She readily accepted. She could count on him to keep up a stream of chatter peppered with amusing antidotes about everyone present, whether true or only supposition on his part. She simply adored the always charming future marquess. He and Marcus Bowen had been Nicholas's closest friends for most of his life and had it not been for those two men remaining tethered to her son during his darkest period, she dared not think what the outcome might have been. For that alone, they would always be family to her.

Huntsleigh leaned down to whisper in her ear as they made their way to the dance floor where partygoers were lining up for one of her favorite country-dances. "A little bird tells me that you have met your new neighbor. Is this true?"

"A little bird?" She arched one eyebrow and smiled up at Spencer. Though she had tried to downplay the event when mentioning it to Marcus, apparently he had seen past her ruse and in turn passed the information on to his wife. She should have known better. "Does this little bird bear a striking resemblance to my lovely daughter-in-law?"

"Indeed it does, how did you know?"

"Hm. And yes, to answer your question, I did run into Mr. Arran Sutherland earlier this morning."

"Ah, but I believe it is Sir, not Mister. It appears the man has been knighted by the crown for his heroics in battle, much as his father was."

The news left her unsettled. She'd had no idea. After their last tryst, she'd not heard from or seen him again. He'd disappeared from her life as if she'd never existed in his. What had happened to him during the thirty years he'd been absent? What had he suffered? What were his triumphs? Had he missed her or thought of her at all?

"I did not know. How wonderful for him."

The opportunity to discover more of what Spencer might know came to an abrupt halt as they took their place on the dance floor, joining four other couples for the quadrille. Too late, she discovered her folly.

"Arran."

His name escaped her, too late to call back and attach the proper address of *Sir* and creating a familiarity that made her blush. But, oh how she loved the sound of his name on her tongue. It came out like a soft breath, a sigh that swept through her entire body.

"Lady Blackbourne. We meet again." Though he did not sound pleased over the encounter.

Her gaze slid to the other couples, Mrs. Farquar and her brother, Jorge. Vicar Ellison and his new wife, Liddy. Had they noticed the coldness in his tone as she had? Her heart ached deep inside her chest.

"Ah, then you are our new-old-almost neighbor." Huntsleigh said. The Ellesmere countryseat, which Spencer would eventually inherit, abutted the opposite side of the Sheridan Park lands than the Sutherland estate. "I was most sorry to hear of your brother's passing. I met the man only once, but I remember I liked him quite well."

"I thank you," Arran said, his voice steady, the deep baritone of it rumbling through her like a thundercloud. "And may I present my niece, Donald's daughter, Miss Judith Sutherland. My sister had hoped to escort her tonight, but fell ill, so I have been given the honor." He smiled at his niece and his formal manner struck Gloria as out of place with the wild, reckless young man she had fallen in love with. The man who had convinced her to run off to Gretna Green, leaving everyone and everything she knew far behind.

She pushed the memory aside and focused on the young lady across from her. She did not stand out in a crowd by any means. Her dress, though well made and of fine material, had been left unadorned of many of the fripperies and frills the other young ladies wore. Her brown hair, though a thick, rich brown that shone in the candlelight had been twisted into a simple knot at the nape of her neck. It was almost as if she did her best not to attract any attention, yet Gloria noted a spark of intelligence in her dark eyes that intrigued her, a reminder that still waters ran deep in the Sutherland family.

"It is lovely to make your acquaintance, my dear."

Miss Sutherland curtsied. "The pleasure is all mine. I must thank you for the kind invitation the Countess of Blackbourne extended to us this day. My family is looking forward to attending your birthday celebrations."

Gloria caught her smile before it could falter. Abigail had failed to mention anything about extending an invitation to the Sutherlands. Apparently her determination to breach the divide between their families had been rewarded. Still, she'd done the right thing. It would have been rude not to invite their neighbors.

"I'm so happy to know you've accepted."

Though the idea of Arran inside Sheridan House left her unsettled. The last time he'd been there, sneaking in during another such party—

No. She would not allow her thoughts to drift there. That memory had no place in her life now.

"I must say, you look quite familiar to me," Huntsleigh added, squinting at Arran as if the connection he sought could be found hidden in the sharpness of his cheekbones or the sternness of his brow.

"I seem to be hearing that sentiment a lot of late."

Did Huntsleigh see it too? Fear trickled through her like ice water in her veins. She saw it, of course. But she knew to look. It lived around his eyes, in the quirk of his mouth when he began to smile, then caught himself. It dwelled in his gestures, his posture, the way he walked into a room. She had not considered it would be noticeable to others. If so, what would it mean?

There was no time to deliberate on the implications as Mr. and Mrs. Quinpers and their son and daughter joined them, giving them their six couples for the quadrille and, after hasty introductions were made, the lively music began. The dance passed in a blur, Gloria's mind working furiously to come to terms with everything that had happened in the short span of a day. The touch of Arran's hand on her gloved one as they met briefly in the middle only served to muddle her thoughts further. Pleasure shot up her arm and made her skin tingle, but it was the intensity behind his gaze when it dropped to the locket around her neck that brought her heart to a shuddering stop.

Did he know what she kept there?

No. How could he?

Blackbourne had made certain of that, hadn't he, ensuring the truth never left her lips, or the tip of her pen. Her letter—a letter she'd thought Arran had received and ignored had been confiscated by her husband and destroyed before it ever left the house. Years later, during one of their many horrible arguments, he'd hurled that fact at her, then threatened if she ever wrote another he would destroy her, Arran, and everyone connected to them.

It had been the same threat he'd used to force her hand into accepting his proposal, promising if she refused him, he would use his power to destroy the Sutherlands, who at the time borrowed heavily, mostly from Blackbourne, to expand their dairy farm. It would take nothing for Blackbourne to call in the loans and destroy them, sending the Sutherlands back from whence they came with nothing more than the clothes on their back. Gloria did not doubt his threats. When Blackbourne wanted something, he did not allow something as small and insignificant as a conscience to get in his way.

When the dance ended, she made her excuses and escaped the crush to step outside the Assembly Rooms and into the cool autumn air with the hope it would restore her. A part of her rejoiced at having Arran so close at hand once again. For years she had pined, knowing nothing would ever come of it. No matter how hard she wished and hoped, he was gone from her life. Lost forever, or so she had thought. Yet, here he was. Returned.

But while one part of her rejoiced, another wept. This Arran was not the young man she had given her love to. This was a man who had weathered the storms of life and been hardened by them. How deep did the scars go? Had the man she'd loved been lost forever by the circumstances he'd lived through? Had the years changed and altered him to such a drastic degree they'd erased all the attributes she'd fallen in love with?

She shook her head and her shoulders drooped. It hardly mattered in the end, did it? His contempt for her was obvious. Any hope that had sprung up upon laying eyes on him earlier was dashed by his cold and brusque manner.

Had the feelings they shared been nothing more than the fleeting infatuation of young love?

No. She refused to believe that. She had loved. Completely and ardently. And forever. It was his memory she'd clung to during the long, bitter years of her marriage to Blackbourne. It was his face she saw whenever she closed her eyes in search of a small moment of happiness. The reminiscence of his touch, his body covering hers, filling her, were the things that had sustained her when she thought she could not bear another day.

"Glory?"

She spun on her heel, her breath lodged in her throat as the phantom of her thoughts materialized in front of her. She said nothing, unsure. If she chose wrongly he might disappear back into the crowded rooms.

He took a step toward her, not stopping until he was close enough to touch. Oh, how she wanted to touch him! She curled her fingers into her palm, then hugged herself tight. For a moment, silence reigned and they simply stood, looking at each other. Into each other.

What did he see? Regret? Despair? Hope? If only she possessed the ability to close her emotions off, keep them from her expression as he did.

"Are you enjoying yourself?" she asked, attempting vainly to distract her thoughts from where they headed.

The corner of his mouth quirked upward before he regained control of it. "As much as one can at such things. Judith and Patience are pleased with the outing, for that I am grateful. They are with Lady Huntsleigh at the moment."

She smiled at the affection in his voice when he mentioned his nieces. "I am happy they came. I look forward to getting to know them. I'm afraid I never had the opportunity to meet Judith before this evening." Blackbourne had forbidden all interaction between her and the Sutherlands.

"Hm," was his only response.

She opened her mouth to explain, but stopped. The time

for explanations in that regard had come and gone and she couldn't find the words to start anew, to make him understand that she had tried. "Will you and Mrs. Sutherland be attending my birthday party?" Abigail had indicated she'd not met his wife during her visit, nor had her name been mentioned during conversation. Curious.

He left the question unanswered, instead surprising her by reaching out, his fingertips lightly brushing the line of her jaw. His brow furrowed, but whatever thoughts went through his head were not revealed on his features. Rivulets of pleasure rushed through her and it took every inch of her will to keep from turning into his touch.

Just as well. He pulled his hand away, as if it had acted independently of the rest of him and surprised them both equally with its recalcitrant behavior.

"You're still very beautiful." He said, tilting his head to one side and studying her, the two lines between his eyebrows deepening. A blush heated her cheeks beneath his intense scrutiny. "I wondered sometimes—"

He stopped and shook his head, as if to dislodge whatever thought he had been about to share with her. Still, the words lingered. *I wondered sometimes.* Had he? As much as she had of him? Daily? More?

His gaze dropped to her chest and he lifted the locket up for closer inspection, resting it in the palm of his hand. How she remembered the feel of those hands upon her skin. Strong and calloused. Despite his family's wealth, Douglas Sutherland did not allow his sons to be idle. How she longed to feel their strength once again, to know the power and safety of his embrace.

She closed her eyes. Having him gone from her life had been a never-ending trial. Having him back in it, without the benefit of how they used to be, agony. She could not say which was worse.

"You still wear this." Though framed as a statement, she heard the question lurking behind it. What did she say? *Yes, it reminds me that I was loved, once. The memory of you—of us—sustains me.*

Did she dare be so bold?

She took a deep breath and tried to find her courage, but years of protecting Arran, of fearing what would happen if the truth were released, stayed her tongue.

"I still wear it." It would have to be enough.

The muscle of his jaw twitched. Was that uncertainty in the deep cobalt blue of his eyes? If so, it lasted only a heartbeat before it disappeared. Perhaps she had only seen what she wished to. A trick of the moon, spurred on by the stars and her silly heart.

"It opens, if I recall."

He pressed a thumb against the clasp, but she stopped him, covering his hand with hers. Warmth spread through her, torturous and delightful. Her heart pounded against her ribs. He gave her a questioning look. A silent request. She acquiesced and released his hand. Her breath caught in her throat as he pushed against the clasp and revealed its secrets. His thumb brushed against the contents with a light touch.

"It's a lock of hair," she said. "Nicholas's."

He gave no indication he'd heard her, only continued to stare at the inky lock of hair curled into the silver heart-shaped interior. Try as she might, she could not read his expression. After a quiet moment, he closed the locket and set it gently back in place. He took a step back, away from her. The small distance created became a chasm, every bit as deep as it was wide.

Oh, how she wished to grab the lapels of his jacket and pull him back. Explain. Whisper the truth into his ear and rejoice in finally setting it free. But his posture brooked no softness, no hint he had any interest in her secrets or justifications, and so she held her ground even while it crumbled beneath her feet.

"You should return to the Assembly Room," he said. "The night grows cold. You'll catch your death if you stay outside."

Except she didn't want to go inside. She did not want to leave him. Not yet. Not like this when there was still so much left unsaid between them. As if sensing her desire, his posture changed, hardened. There would be no breaching the divide this night. Perhaps not any night.

"Good evening, my lady." He bowed and turned away from her, walking further out into the night to where the candlelight from the Assembly Room no longer reached him and left him shrouded in shadows.

"You should have told him," she whispered, unable to stop the sheen of tears that caused his retreating image to waver until he disappeared completely.

But how? And to what end?

Chapter Four

"You look like the picture of health," Arran said as Beatris breezed into the morning room, color blooming in her cheeks and a smile lighting her face. "Fully recovered are we?"

He could not prevent the sarcasm from edging into his inquiry.

She ignored it. "Indeed. I feel most restored after a night's rest. Did you enjoy yourself last night?"

He gave her a look. Not a happy one, though she received it with a light laugh, then proceeded to fix herself a small plate from the buffet table.

In truth, he could not remember the evening with much clarity. Every minute that came after his meeting with Glory had occurred in some blurry netherworld between confusion and anger and crazy, irrational hope.

Why did she wear his locket? It didn't make any sense. Surely she had other pieces—more expensive and ostentatious baubles—she could have chosen. Perhaps, if it had been only the one time, he could toss it off. Women of her ilk had plenty of trinkets to choose from. Likely her lady's maid had selected it and she thought nothing of it. Had forgotten its significance over the years. Did not even recall who had given it to her. *If* it had been only once. But it hadn't been.

She would have changed and dressed for the evening's entertainment. To choose to wear the locket again, after changing from one outfit to another, indicated a conscious decision on her part. But why? What did it mean? And why a lock of her son's hair? Did she mean to mock him with it? To remind him Blackbourne had taken everything from him, even going so far as to taint his gift to her in such a way?

His thoughts had troubled him long into the night, making for a very restless sleep and when he finally succumbed, she haunted him there as well, so that he was afforded no respite from the suffering of seeing her in the flesh once again.

How he wanted her. Still. Instantly. Desperately. Despite everything she had done to him, abandoning him in favor of a titled lord who thought of her as nothing more than a pretty possession to be strutted about like a prized mare.

Beatris took a seat next to him at the round table near the window and glanced at his plate. "You have not touched your breakfast, brother dear."

"I find myself lacking in appetite this morning."

"Patience indicated Lady Blackbourne attended the Assembly last night. I must confess I am sorry to have missed that. It has been years since I have seen her, although my lovely daughter informed me that the Dowager Countess has aged remarkably well and rivaled the beauty of any of the younger women who attended. I can't help but think my dear girl was suggesting a comparison to her old mother and found me lacking in that regard."

"I am sure she meant nothing of the sort," he said, without acknowledging anything regarding Glory, her presence, or the effect it had on him even hours after their encounter.

"Please, we both know where Patience's values lie. Heavens, but I do not know where I went wrong with that child." Beatris shook her head and took a small bite from her buttered biscuit.

"You allowed your husband to spoil her within an inch of her life."

"Hm. Daughters have a knack for being able to wrap their fathers around their little finger."

Arran peered at his sister over the edge of the morning paper. "Spoken from experience, I assume?"

She smiled, a sly, knowing grin that always made him nervous. "Don't think I haven't noticed your avoiding my inquiry about Lady Blackbourne."

He scowled. The woman possessed the uncanny ability to divine information from the smallest things. A truly annoying trait, in his humble opinion.

"Was there an inquiry?"

"You know there was. Did you speak with her?"

Arran straightened and raised the newspaper. "Did I not forbid this particular topic?"

"And have you not noticed how awful I am at taking such dictates from my little brother?"

He sighed. He should have known Beatris would not hold her tongue forever. Raised amongst three boys, two older and one younger, she had quickly filled the role of mother to them upon the death of their own and was quite nimble-footed when it came to maneuvering around them to get her own way.

Perhaps Elmsley wasn't completely to blame for Patience's behavior, after all. Perhaps she had learned too well at her mother's knee. Despite that, he did not hold such things against his sister. When Mother had died, Beatris had stepped up to fill the role as best she could, despite being but four and ten at the time. But her role was short-lived when, less than a handful of years later, Baron Elmsley expressed an interest. Soon, his only sister married and Arran was left alone once again. As the heir and the spare, Boyd and Donald held their father's full attention, while he...well, he'd had Glory's, hadn't he?

He cleared his throat and folded the paper, pushing the thought away. "If you must know, yes, Lady Blackbourne was indeed at the Assembly and, yes, we spoke briefly. But I am sorry to disappoint, it was all terribly civilized and uneventful." Save for when he touched her face, her soft skin burning against his own and creating a need so deep and visceral he had yet to shake it.

"On the contrary, I am most pleased to hear this. It means you will have no excuse to avoid her upcoming birthday party."

He clenched his jaw, certain he had just backed into the trap his sister had cleverly set for him. "I am quite certain I will be indisposed that evening."

"I am afraid you cannot be. You see, Elmsley has sent word he is in need of my presence in London. Some important dinner with the Duke of Franklyn that cannot be missed and for which my attendance is required. He believes they may be eyeing dear Charlie as a husband for Lady Susan. It would be quite the boon if our son could nab himself a duke's daughter and I simply cannot pass up the opportunity presented."

"I fail to see what that has to do with me or my attending Lady Blackbourne's birthday party." Nor did he want to see. What he wanted was for the subject of his former lover to be dropped. Was it not enough that she plagued his dreams? Must she also permeate his waking moments as well?

Not that he needed his sister to assist in that regard.

"Allow me to enlighten you. Given Patience's rather...

eventful first Season—" Beatris cleared her throat, and her expression became that of a beleaguered mother whose daughter had inherited her own strong will, much to her detriment. "—I believe it best she remains out of London for the time being, until the memory of the ton grows short. However, the party for Lady Blackbourne is likely to bring about many eligible gentlemen and well-placed lords and ladies that Patience will benefit from getting to know—under proper supervision, that is."

"Such proper supervision being me, I take it?"

"I knew you would agree."

"I have agreed to no such thing."

"Then you may be the one to tell her, and Judith, that the party they have been looking forward to will have to be missed. I don't have the heart to do it myself. Especially after I have seen the excitement in their lovely faces upon informing them you would, naturally, escort them in my place."

"You didn't."

His sister's smile grew wider. "Oh, but I did."

"Hell and damnation, Bea!"

"Language." She leaned back in her chair, a look of satisfaction upon her pleasant features. "Now don't get your back up. After all, you loved each other once, did you not?"

"I—we—that is—" Words sputtered out of him at his sister's blunt question, but none of them made any sense. She waved him off.

"And you are now both widowed and practically living next door to each other. I think it a most fortuitous twist of fate, do you not?"

"I do not." He found it anything but fortuitous. He found it maddening. Agonizing. Terrifying.

"Pish. She is a lovely woman. Everyone says as much. I see no reason for you to hold onto past hurts. It's like you've used them to build an iron cage around your heart and I can think of nothing more tragic."

He could. Losing her all over again would be far more tragic. It would be devastating. Soul-crushing. He wouldn't survive it a second time. He'd barely survived the first.

"Put away your romantic notions, Beatris. You may play matchmaker for your children, but not me. She and I were not meant to be then, and nothing has changed in the thirty odd years since our association ended."

Beatris stood and made to leave, stopping in front of him on her way to the door. "Except that it has never really ended, has it?"

She did not wait for his reply. Nor did he have one to give her. No. That was a lie. He did have an answer. He simply lacked the courage to admit it.

"A crow? Called Shadow? What an odd thing." Nicholas set down the newspaper and took a sip of coffee, his expression less reminiscent of the Earl of Blackbourne and more like the young boy Gloria had raised —one with a habit of questioning anything that sounded even remotely curious.

"Yes. A crow. Quite tame, to tell the truth." She wasn't sure what possessed her to speak of Callum to Nicholas. Her intention had been to let the matter be. But as she sat down to enjoy an early breakfast with her son, the story popped out, as if it had a will of its own.

"Would a boy not prefer a dog?"

"I suppose not in this instance. Although his father had always favored dogs and likely has at least one, so I assume he is not lacking in that respect. But the bird seems quite taken with the boy and he, it. There was something quite charming

about it." She smiled. Her brief meeting with Callum Sutherland had left an impression on her, one that had lingered in
the days since she found him calling for his crow to come
down from the tree.

"He must be quite the young fellow to be able to
command the respect of a bird who could simply fly away if it
chose to, never to return," the Earl of Glenmor commented.

Abigail's brother, Benedict, had arrived late the previous
day to spend time with his younger sister and new nephew and
to attend Gloria's birthday party the following week. He'd
brought with him his mother, Lorena. Gloria had never been
more thankful to see her dear friend. She could use a sympa-
thetic shoulder that did not belong to one of her children. The
matter that plagued her was not for their ears.

After her unexpected encounter with Arran outside of the
Assembly, she could not settle. Worries and fears whirled
about inside of her, tangled with need and desire. Her feelings
for Arran had not diminished over the years, nor did she
expect them to any time in the near future. Being in such close
proximity did not help matters. She supposed she could leave
for London, but she had always preferred the country and had
no wish to return to the city more than was necessary.

Nicholas's voice interrupted her thoughts. "I would like to
meet this crow-tamer. Perhaps he can talk some sense into
young Roddy, who seems to think screaming at the top of his
lungs in the middle of the night is perfectly acceptable
behavior for a young viscount. Why I found my poor wife
leaning against a shelf in the library napping on her feet yester-
day, so exhausted is she after a week of getting up through the
night to tend to him."

"Is that not what the nanny is for?" Benedict took a bite of
coddled eggs.

"Indeed, it is. However, Abigail has determined that when
Roddy cries, he is not expecting to see a stranger's face, but

that of his mother's and so off she goes." Nicholas made a shooing motion with his hand.

Gloria smiled at the men. "It is the way of mothers to nurture their young. We do not hand over the care of them easily to another, no matter how exhausted we become."

Benedict lowered his fork. "Even if you find yourself sleeping against a bookshelf?"

She laughed. "Even then." How she missed those days now. Difficult as they had been at the time, at least she'd had a purpose. There had been nothing she wouldn't have done for her son. She would have given up everything.

She had given up everything.

Her smile faltered.

"Perhaps we should pay Sir Arran a visit, Nick. What say you?" Benedict suggested.

Gloria choked on a sip of warm chocolate. "Oh no. No. That would be..." She cleared her throat and worked to regain the composure that had slipped away at the notion of Nicholas and Benedict descending upon Arran's home.

"Mother?"

"It is just that...well, I imagine they are still in mourning after Mr. Sutherland's passing."

Nicholas gave her a questioning look. "But were they not at the Assembly last night?"

"Well...yes."

"And did Abby not invite them to your birthday party, an invitation they readily accepted?"

"They did." Her voice weakened along with her argument.

"Then it is settled," Benedict said, his hand tapping against the pristine white tablecloth. "Shall we ride out this morning? The sun is bright in the sky and it is destined to be the perfect day to be out of doors."

In the time she had known Abigail's brother, Gloria had noted he often looked for any excuse to be outside as opposed to in. Lorena suggested it was likely a response to his sudden elevation to Earl of Glenmor and the near crippling debt that had come with the title and properties. His mother suspected the fresh air made him feel a little less stifled. It was a tactic Gloria had oft employed herself and one she fully understood and endorsed.

Realizing there was nothing more she could do to stop them, she managed a small smile and prayed Arran was not at home to receive them. "Then please send my best regards to the Sutherlands."

As the gentlemen excused themselves to depart for their journey to the Sutherland lands, Gloria pushed away her untouched plate of food, her appetite extinguished in the face of Nicholas's plan to visit the man she had given up for her son's sake.

And for the sake of the man they planned to meet.

Chapter Five

"Father? There are riders heading this way. Do you think they are lost?" Callum's eyes grew wide as he peered over at Arran, a gleam of adventure mirrored within them. "Highwaymen, perhaps? Shall Shadow and I run them off?"

"I sincerely doubt they are highwaymen and I strongly suggest you stay put." He had taken Callum out for a ride on the new horse he'd recently purchased for him. His son had a strange ability to understand animals and the gentle thorough-bred had taken to him from the beginning. "What would they think, to see you charging down upon them? With Shadow perched on your shoulder, they may well think you were Death coming to call."

Callum grinned, inordinately pleased by this. Arran tried, without success, to suppress a smile as he squinted in the direction of the riders approaching them. There were three in total, none of whom he recognized. Then again, with his long absence, very few from the village and surrounding estates looked familiar any more. They advanced at a good clip as if they were racing one another to see who could reach him first.

"Stay here." He issued the order as he pushed his heels into his mare and rode ahead. As the men grew closer, he confirmed he had not become acquainted with any of them, though two looked familiar and he suspected he had seen them at the Assembly the previous night.

He pulled up on the reins and heard Shadow's caw much closer than it should have been had his son heeded his dictate and remained higher up on the hill where he had left him. He glanced over his shoulder.

Callum shrugged. "I could not help it, Father. Shadow wanted to see who they were."

Arran shook his head and hid his smile. The boy had inherited the Sutherland's strong will to do as he pleased.

"A-ha!" The tallest of the three announced, grinning at the other two who flanked either side of him. "I have bested you yet again!"

The man to Arran's right with sharp features and dark hair addressed the other, his tone riddled in wryness. "You have cheated, once again, and I consider your claim forfeit."

"How did I cheat?"

The man to the far left answered. "You took off before we were even in the saddle. And before you debate the issue, might I suggest we greet this other gentleman before he is convinced we possess not a single manner amongst us?"

The man in the middle grinned and Arran's heart leaped to his throat as the late morning sunlight glinted against the man's silvery eyes, revealing his identity before he gave his name.

"Forgive us. Allow me to introduce myself. I am—"

"Nicholas Sheridan, the Earl of Blackbourne," Arran said.

Blackbourne straightened in his seat. "Yes. Have we met before?"

Arran shook his head. "No. We have not." *You have your mother's eyes.*

"Are you certain?" The dark-haired man with the sharp features leaned forward in his saddle, his piercing gaze penetrating deep. "You do look quite familiar."

Why did everyone keep saying that? It wasn't as if he favored either of his brothers. They had taken after his father's side—short and squat, while he resembled his mother's taller and leaner side of the family.

"I attended last night's Assembly briefly. Perhaps you saw me there." He had not stayed long after his brief rendezvous with Glory. Patience had not been pleased at their early departure, but he'd promised to make it up to his nieces. Unfortunately, that would likely mean taking them to Glory's birthday ball, thanks to his sister's machinations.

God help him.

"Perhaps that is it." But the other man did not look convinced.

"Either way," Blackbourne said. "It is my pleasure to introduce my two brothers-in-law. Fine gentlemen both, although less accomplished riders, as we have just witnessed. This—" He waved to the dark-haired man. "—is Mr. Marcus Bowen, who has had the great fortune of marrying my lovely sister. His estate resides just over yonder. And my other companion is Benedict Laytham, the Earl of Glenmor, my wife's brother."

Arran nodded at the gentlemen. "Pleased to meet you. I am Sir Arran Sutherland. This young man who has crept up behind me is my son, Callum."

Shadow cawed in response.

"Ah," Glenmor said, looking over Arran's shoulder. "The infamous crow-tamer. Lady Blackbourne speaks quite highly of you."

The idea Glory spoke of Callum to another, highly or otherwise, surprised him. A part of him wanted to believe she possessed a callous heart, despite all the evidence he had seen and heard in the past two days to the contrary. It left him unsettled. He'd clung to this conviction for so long to explain her sudden change of heart, that he felt somewhat off-center without it. What other explanation could there be for the way she had heartlessly tossed him aside for another, abandoning the promises they had made as if they meant nothing?

"Did she truly say that?" Callum's proud smile doing little to ease a sudden, strange anxiety that surged within Arran.

"She did, indeed," Blackbourne said. "May I see him up close?"

The earl dismounted the black thoroughbred he rode and strode toward Callum. Arran watched his movements, tried to find the similarities between the man who approached his son and the woman he had loved all those years ago. *Still did.* But aside from the pale, silvery eyes, he found nothing. And yet, there was something familiar about him—but the harder he tried to grasp what it was, the more elusive it became.

"His name is Shadow."

"A very appropriate name, I would think. May I pet him, or will he nip my finger off?" Blackbourne leaned in closer to Callum and lifted one dark eyebrow, his expression almost conspiratorial. "I'm rather fond of my fingers. I would hate to lose one."

"I think you should be safe. He mostly likes shiny baubles. Oh!" Callum sat upright and dug into the pocket of his jacket. Shadow crowed sharply at the sudden movement and Blackbourne took a quick step back.

Glenmor laughed. "The great horseman afraid of a small bird."

Mr. Bowen shook his head. "Indeed. They shall tell this story for ages to come."

Blackbourne shot his two companions a dark look to which they responded with innocent gazes as if they had done nothing wrong. The close bonds between the three was evident, something Arran had missed himself growing up with the gap in ages between he and his brothers. Even while in the military, his position of authority required he maintained a certain distance between himself and his men.

Callum held out his hand toward Blackbourne, the ring Glory had given him catching the sunlight. "I forgot to give this to Father last night to return to Lady Blackbourne. She allowed me to use it when Shadow refused to come down from a tree. Would you mind?"

"Not at all." Blackbourne smiled and reached for the ring.

Shadow, however, had other ideas about giving up his treasure. He cawed again and plucked the bauble from Callum's hand.

"Ah!" Blackbourne jumped back once again, nearly unseating Mr. Bowen and Glenmor, who could not have found the scene more amusing.

"Oh, uh..." Callum twisted his mouth to one side, a guilty expression clouding his elfish features.

"You know," Blackbourne said, straightening his riding coat and, likely his ego as well, given the way he glowered at his two friends. "Mother has more baubles than she wears. In truth, aside from her locket, I rarely see her wear most of them. I'm certain she is in no hurry to have the ring returned."

"Especially if it means Nick might return home with one less finger," Mr. Bowen suggested. "In truth, the purpose of our visit was not jewel retrieval, but, as your neighbors, to introduce ourselves."

"Very...neighborly of you," Arran said, unsure of how to respond to the onslaught of attention. He had grown into a solitary sort, a way of life that had suited his position in the military and his injured heart. And after that, perhaps it had simply become habit. When one held themselves at bay from others, they were less likely to be disappointed. Betrayed. Abandoned.

Even his marriage had been based on this premise, a truth

he loathed to acknowledge, but one he could no longer refute now that he had come face to face with Glory once again. Her arrival back in his life resurrected old fears and made it impossible to ignore the fact that when he'd married Jean, he'd chosen a good woman he would never love. Not truly.

His heart had been too damaged to open to another. Jean had deserved more from him. Though she never complained, she had to have known his heart belonged to another. That she put up with him and continued to treat him with kindness and friendship was far more than he had deserved from her, and a true testament to her forgiving nature. Thankfully, Callum had inherited his mother's kind and open nature.

"Might we ride along with you?" Blackbourne suggested, breaking the silence that had fallen between them. "I am most interested to hear about what you have planned for the estate. Perhaps we can help each other. I do love a good collaboration."

"Capital idea," Glenmor agreed and, much as Arran would have preferred to continue on his solitary ride with only the company of his son, he could not find a way to extricate himself from the trio of men who had descended upon them. Besides, should he deny their request, he would then have to suffer through a proper scolding from his sister about manners and such upon her return from London. He preferred to avoid such a rebuke even more than he wished to avoid the company of Blackbourne and his companions.

And, though he would never admit such a thing aloud, he wanted to learn more about Glory, about what she had done over the past three decades and why, according to her son, the only piece of jewelry she wore with any regularity was the locket he had given her shortly before she destroyed his heart.

He forced a smile, or a reasonable facsimile of one. "Very well, then. Come along."

"I do not require a new gown for the party. I have a wardrobe full of gowns created by Mrs. Bell that were made just before your father's passing, none of which have yet been worn. Any one of them would be adequate." Gloria let the fine, printed silk slide through her fingers as she addressed her daughter.

Rebecca threw her arms up as far as her afternoon dress would allow and let her gloved hands slap against her thighs, her pretty features taking on a rather militant slant. "*Mother*, those gowns are nearly two years out of fashion. This is a party in *your* honor to celebrate *your* birthday. I know you are not the extravagant sort, but I do not think this one time it is out of the ordinary to expect you would put a little effort into going above and beyond the everyday."

"She does have a point," Lorena said, touching the lovely cornflower blue silk with pinstripes of silver shot through it. "It would not hurt to treat yourself."

"It is wasteful," she shrugged. After Blackbourne's death, the strict dictates of his will brought her and Rebecca to the brink of financial ruin. The threat of being dependent upon Nicholas to support them while the bulk of the late earl's unentailed fortune went to his mistress hung over their heads like a guillotine with its blade poised to fall. The prospect had left an indelible impression on Gloria. When one came within a hair's breadth of becoming a poor relation, extravagance lost its appeal. A new dress held no importance.

"I will agree to having one of Mrs. Bell's gowns altered for the party, but that is all."

"Then what about a new piece of jewelry," Rebecca suggested. "A lovely choker, perhaps?"

Gloria lifted a hand to her locket, as if to protect it from Rebecca's suggestion. Barely a day had passed in the last three decades when she hadn't worn it and on those few occasions when she hadn't, she'd felt naked without it. "Perhaps something for my hair, instead," she suggested, hoping to appease her daughter and Lorena.

"Perfect!" I am going to skip next door to Mr. Bremmer's shop and pick something out for you. It is the only way I can ensure you will not change your mind."

Rebecca dropped a quick kiss on Gloria's cheek and hurried from the dress shop, likely afraid if she lingered, Gloria would change her mind. Lorena's light laughter trickled around her. "Never get in the way of a well-meaning daughter on a mission, I always say."

Gloria smiled and shook her head. "She means well, of that I have no doubt, but I truly do not need more than what I have. I am perfectly content. I shall leave playing lady of the manor and all that entails to Abigail. Your daughter is much more suited to the task. And heaven knows, she has far more support in Nicholas than I ever had with Blackbourne."

Lorena reached out and gave Gloria's hand a brief squeeze. "And what shall you do with your time now? Continue to travel?"

The idea held no appeal. Even less now that Arran had returned to take over the Sutherland estate. His presence somehow rooted her, entangling her in the dream she had clung to all these years. That he would return; that they would have a second chance. Such an irrational notion given his obvious feelings toward her, or lack thereof. "No, I think I shall take up residence in the Dowager House and live a quiet, uneventful life."

But she could not work up any enthusiasm for her plans. Something about them felt so...empty. Lonely. Unless...

She shook her head.

"What is it?" Lorena drew closer. "You have not been yourself these past two days since my return. Abigail and

Rebecca have mentioned it as well, and I can see they were right."

Gloria took a deep breath and looked around. The shop had quieted with only a few patrons perusing the ready-made dresses and bolts of fabric on the other side of the room. "It is Sir Arran Sutherland."

"Your new neighbor?"

"Old neighbor, actually, though it's been nigh on thirty years and a bit since I saw him last, at least until the other day."

"And your re-introduction did not go well?"

Oh, how to explain. No one beyond Arran's family, her own, and Blackbourne had known of their relationship and she had been happy to keep it that way, all things considered. But now, with his return, all the feelings she'd tried so hard to hide raged forward and brought with them a chorus of need and desire she had not experienced since their last time together.

"It is only that...you see..." She pursed her lips.

"Gloria Sheridan," Lorena lowered her voice and drew closer still. "Do you have feelings for Sir Arran?"

"I...I..."

"You do! Oh, this is so grand!"

"No! No, it is not grand. It is not grand at all. In fact, it is nothing short of a disaster. He has no interest in me whatso-ever. Time has ensured his heart has turned bitter toward me and I suppose I cannot blame him. He thinks I threw him over to marry Blackbourne, and he is right in a sense. Besides, he has a son and is married—"

"But Abigail mentioned there was no Mrs. Sutherland present or spoken of when she visited."

Gloria had also noticed Arran's reticence to answer her own inquiries in that regard. "Yes, but—"

The jingle of the bell on the shop door interrupted her and she looked up. Blinked. It could not be.

"Oh my..." Lorena breathed and her hand fluttered at her chest.

As if sensing her presence, Arran turned and Gloria experienced the full power of his potent gaze as it burned through her from tip to toe. Good Lord above, did the man have any idea the effect he had on her? The way it awakened everything inside of her?

Arran hesitated at the threshold, indecision stamped across his handsome features as if debating whether to acknowledge her with a nod and walk on, or do the polite thing and stop to offer a greeting. Politeness evidently won out and he moved toward them.

Lorena's grip on Gloria's hand tightened, a fact she became aware of only once it hit a painful squeeze.

Arran executed a brief bow. "Good morning, Lady Blackbourne."

"Sir Arran. I trust the day finds you well?" Her heart thudded in her chest and she rushed on. "May I present my dear friend, Mrs. Laytham, the current Lady Blackbourne's mother."

"Ah." Arran bowed again. "I am pleased to make your acquaintance. I had the great pleasure of meeting your daughter recently. A delightful lady to be sure."

"How thoughtful of you to say. She mentioned her visit with you and your sister, Lady Elmsley. She did not mention meeting Mrs. Sutherland, however. Did she not make the trip from Dumfries with you?"

Gloria forced herself not to kick her dear friend in the ankle for her blatant inquiry. Leave it to Lorena to get straight to the heart of the matter.

"Mrs. Sutherland passed on two years ago, I'm afraid. It is just Callum and I now."

Her heart stuttered first before racing on ahead, awakening the hope she had tried so hard to quash. He was widowed! Her joy over this fact no doubt earning her a rather prominent spot in Hell. She issued a silent apology to the late Mrs. Sutherland. If Callum favored his mother, she must have been a lovely lady and did not deserve to depart this world so early before seeing her only child grow into adulthood.

Lorena put a hand to her heart. "I am most sorry to hear of your loss. Well, look at us. All three widowed and far too young for such a state. In fact, I was just saying to Lady Blackbourne how it seems a shame for her to hole up inside the Dowager House as if she had nothing left to offer the world. Don't you agree, Sir Arran?"

Forget kicking her *dear friend* in the ankle. A gag around her mouth would be a much preferable punishment.

"I am certain Sir Arran has much better things to do than to comment on the state of my affairs."

"As it is," he said, "I am tasked with the job of picking up the items my nieces have ordered for your birthday fete. They are both looking forward to the event. I'm certain it has been the only thing Patience has spoken of since the invitation was issued."

"And you, Sir Arran?" Lorena smiled and looped her arm through Gloria's. Her friend was enjoying this conversation far too much. "Will you be attending as well?"

"Indeed. My sister has been called back to London and has requested my assistance in offering to chaperone the young ladies."

Lorena smiled and hugged Gloria's arm closer to her. "How lovely! We certainly look forward to seeing you there."

Arran nodded at Lorena before his gaze drifted to Gloria and stayed, piercing through her for the length of several heartbeats before it dropped to her locket then quickly skittered away to the front of the store. "Well, I must make my apologies. If I do not return with all due haste, I fear my nieces will send out a search party for me. I bid you both a good day."

It wasn't until he left for the front of the shop that Gloria pulled Lorena outside with great hurry and gulped the cool October air in an attempt to restore herself.

"Well he is a fine, *fine* specimen of—"

"Lorena!"

"What?" Lorena blinked innocently. "I was going to say *gentleman*. A fine specimen of gentleman. Now," she took Gloria's arm once more and led her toward Mr. Bremmer's shop. "When we return home, I insist you tell me every last detail about your past with Sir Arran."

"There is nothing to tell." *There is too much to tell.*

"Nonsense. The heat between the two of you nearly set my hems on fire."

"Good heavens, Lorena! The things you say."

Her friend threw her head back and laughed, drawing the attention of several villagers, though Lorena cared little. Gloria wished she had the same sense of self-acceptance, but her past had been too steeped in conforming her behavior to suit others.

The one time she'd tried to break away from such expectations, she'd paid a terrible price.

Chapter Six

Arran pulled up on the reins of his horse and peered over the expanse of land belonging to the Earl of Blackbourne. The *new* Earl of Blackbourne. How odd to come to the realization the life he had left behind had marched on in his absence. In his mind, it had remained stagnant. Tattered. Broken.

And yet it wasn't.

Glory was no longer the girl who had broken his heart. She had aged with the years just as he had, though instead of fading, her beauty had matured. Deepened. But something else within her had changed. Something that went far deeper than the surface. He could see it in her eyes, a ravaged pain and inherent strength resided there, as if she had survived a war, much as he had.

Her children were now adults in their own right, older even than he and Glory were when they had fallen in love and promised each other a future that never came to be. How eager they had been back then to take on the world and society and prove to everyone that nothing could destroy their love.

How wrong they had been.

Or had they? She still wore his locket. Still looked at him as she had when they were young and believed in love. He saw it whenever she glanced his way, her expression a mix of...of what? Need, desire. Love? How difficult it was to see this and not gather her in his arms and hold her tight, to make promises that this time it would be different. This time, he would not let her go.

Fool. Years had passed. An entire lifetime. She had borne children who had grown. They had both married others and watched as their respective spouses passed on to leave them alone once more. Did she miss Blackbourne upon his passing? Had she mourned the earl? Had she loved him in the end?

His heart withered at the idea of it. He ought to let it go. He *needed* to let it go. Yet three days had passed since seeing her at the dress shop and still each morning he rode out to this very spot where he first saw her once again, hoping...

For what?

A second chance.

No. He did not believe in second chances. He'd learned during his years in the war the finality of things. Second chances were rarely ever granted, whether deserved or not.

Did he deserve one? Did she?

A twig snapped and he glanced toward the copse of woods to his left. A moment later, Glory rode out from the shadows, oblivious to his presence. He sat still in the saddle and watched her, a vision of loveliness defined by the autumn colors that surrounded her and the pale sunlight that lit her ivory skin. She closed her eyes and lifted her face to greet it. Her chest rose and fell as she breathed it in and a small smile touched the corners of her mouth. He nudged his horse and rode down to greet her before his better sense could counsel him to leave, return to the manor. Forget he had ever seen her.

She turned upon his approach and for a brief second her smile faltered. Perhaps his better sense had been correct. He should have been content to simply gaze upon her. But the rest of him, the parts that had longed for her year after year—longed for her still—continued to ignore any sense at all.

"Good morning, Glory." Glory. He smiled at the name. She had never cared for the one given her at birth, but he had loved it. It was more than fitting, as he had never met a woman more glorious than she. And so he had shortened it, telling her that to him, she was a glory.

Her smile resurrected itself and with it a glint of hope in her eyes, which sent his heart soaring. He treaded dangerous ground riddled with traps and pitfalls. If he'd been on the battlefield, he'd be a goner for certain. His heart pumped with desire and yet cringed with fear. He had not given his heart since the last time it had been broken. Did he even remember how? Did it matter?

Glory broke the pregnant silence between them. "Were you waiting for me?"

"No." He hadn't been waiting, he'd simply been hoping.

"I see." She stared at him and her gaze seeped through to where his heart cowered in his chest and wrapped around it, enveloping it with a gentle touch. He let out a slow breath. "Shall I carry on then?"

He nodded but his words contradicted him. "No."

She rested her hands and the reins in her lap and looked at him with expectation, as if they were playing a game of chess and the next move was his. He'd never been a very good chess player. Subterfuge and strategy were all well and good on the battlefield of war, but this was a different arena altogether, and not one he excelled at. He had waded out of his depth and lost sight of the shore.

Again, she proved braver than he. "Would you care to walk with me for a bit?"

He had stacks of work awaiting him back at his study. Convoluted piles of ledgers that Judith had done her best to keep up during her father's long illness that needed his attention. None of which appealed to him at the moment. In this moment, he wanted only to gaze upon Glory's beauty, swim through the memories of their past and reach for her like a lifeline thrown to a drowning sailor.

"I think I would like that very much."

Arran dismounted and hobbled his horse near a thick patch of grass that had not yet browned from the cooler temperatures, then returned to assist Glory down from her mare, lifting her from the sidesaddle and slowly lowering her to the ground. The skirts of her riding habit did little to tamp down the riot created inside of him as her body brushed against his.

Aside from their encounter at the Assembly, this was the closest he had been to her since sneaking into her room at Sheridan Park all those years ago. How reckless they had been then. How reckless he felt now with her soft curves molded against his hands and his body demanding he pull her against him and hold her close until everything wrong was put right again. As if that was all it took. Just holding her. He closed his eyes. Maybe instinct had the right of it. Maybe that *was* all it took. If he simply let go. Gave in.

He took a breath. She smelled of freshly bloomed daisies. She always had.

Her gloved hand touched his face and he opened his eyes to find her peering up at him with those damnable silvery eyes, a slightly darker shade than her son's, warmer and completely unforgettable. How they had haunted his dreams. Continued to still.

She did not move away and he lacked the ability to do so himself.

"I don't know why I came here today," he said. A lie. He'd come for the same reason he'd come here every day since first seeing her again. At first, he'd told himself it was to remind him of all the reasons he had to despise her, but his reasoning failed when each time he saw her, or each time someone mentioned her name and sang her praises he was reminded all over again why he had loved her so deeply.

He'd painted her the villain in his mind, but the more he tried to focus on the picture now, the more incomplete it became. Edges were smudged and blurry, the colors wrong, the dimensions distorted.

"I'm glad you came." She smiled and his insides did that thing where they took flight like a hundred pairs of wings flitting around in his belly. "I am always happy to see you."

Her words struck him. Confused him. "You are?"

"You have been gone much too long. I have missed you horribly." The words whispered from her and brushed against his skin like a caress, but they did nothing to settle his confusion. She had sent him away. Threw him over for another. Even when he came back, determined to convince her to leave her husband and run off with him, she had accepted him into her bed but then banished him from her life.

Had she regretted her decision? Wished she'd chosen differently?

"But you—"

She shook her head and slid her hand over his jaw until the tips of her fingers covered his mouth. "I don't want to talk about the past. It is too painful and we have both suffered enough for it, have we not? I know you have only just returned and that in the years past you have married and now mourn your wife, who I am certain must have been a lovely woman, but I—"

She stopped and her eyes glistened with unshed tears, mesmerizing him. He had pictured this moment repeatedly. Day in and day out. Year upon year, decade over decade. Yet in his scenario, she begged his forgiveness, pleaded with him to take her back, to rescue her from the bitterness of marriage to a man that would never be his equal. A part of him still wanted that. Needed to hear it.

Ego.

He wrapped his fingers around her narrow wrist and freed his mouth. "What do you want from me?" Did she expect them to pick up where they had left off? Pretend as if nothing had happened?

She gave him a tentative smile, like the one he remembered so fondly from their first meeting. "I think I would very much like you to kiss me."

Her boldness startled him and he did not respond. Did not know how. There was nothing he wanted more. Nothing he *feared* more, because one kiss would never be enough. It never was where she was concerned. It had been his downfall, his Waterloo.

Color bloomed in her cheeks and she dropped her gaze. "Forgive me," she whispered. "How inappropriate of me. I should never have made such a—"

He didn't let her finish. He tilted her chin and captured her mouth with his before he had time to think beyond what he did. What he wanted. Needed. And oh yes, he needed this. With everything inside of him, he needed this. Her mouth, soft and pliable, against his. Hungry, searching. Desperate. As if she could not get enough of him. Or he, her. Nothing had changed.

Everything has changed.

He didn't care. Not now. Not in this moment. In this moment, he only needed her. Her taste, her tongue, her lips. The scent of daisies swirling around them like an aphrodisiac he could never resist. He pulled her closer. Held her tighter. Kissed her harder.

Behind her, her mare neighed and snorted, a shot of reality into a delightful fantasy where she belonged to him once again. But he did not live in dreams. He could not afford to.

He broke the kiss and took a step back, her mouth, red and swollen enticing him to return. He averted his gaze to the tree standing tall in the distance behind her.

"Forgive me." He cleared his throat, collected his rattled senses. "I took liberties I should not have."

"You did nothing I did not ask you to." Her words were breathless, the color in her cheeks burned now from a different source. Passion. Desire. How he had forgotten the feeling. The way those emotions looked upon her features. The destruction they employed.

"This was a mistake." He shook his head and took another step back, needing distance to clear his head. And his heart. "I will assist you in mounting your horse then I must be on my way."

He could not stay. He could not resist her and he could not be responsible for what he would do if he did not send her away.

"Arran?" She said his name and a question lingered behind it, yet he had no answers to give her. No way to frame what the devastation of losing her had done to him. Would do to him again. And even if he did, he would not tell her. He didn't want to give her that kind of power.

No. It wasn't that. She already had the power. He simply did not want her to know she did. One did not give the enemy the upper hand. But was she the enemy? The question lingered and taunted no matter how hard he tried to banish it.

"This will never work." His hand moved back and forth between them. "Our time is over." It should not hurt so much to say these words. Yet it did. Deep and cleaving as if he had carved out a piece of his heart only to watch it die.

She stood firm, though her voice wavered and it was the latter that nearly proved his undoing. He hated to see her pain. Even now. Even after all she had done to destroy him. "Why can it not be again? Would it not be worth exploring? Do we not owe each other at least that?"

Her words took him aback, reminded him of why this could never be. "Owe each other?" What did he owe her? She had tossed him aside the minute someone with a lofty title and deep pockets came along. She had traded him in as if he meant nothing in exchange for pomp and circumstance and got exactly what she wanted. What she deserved. He owed her nothing!

"We loved each other once," she said.

"Once." He held his anger in front of him like a shield. "But once was a long time ago. Forgive me, my lady, but I really cannot tarry here any longer. If you will allow me to assist you onto your mount, I will bid you adieu. And I believe, in future, we should refrain from such meetings, inadvertent or otherwise."

He did not meet her gaze direct, but he could sense her searching for it. After a long, silent moment, she stopped and he reached out to lift her back onto her mare, careful to keep her away from him as much as possible. Once she was upon the saddle, he waited until she adjusted her leg over the pommel then handed her the reins.

"Arran," she tried again, but he shook his head, cutting her off. He balanced on a thin thread tangled between what he knew and what he wanted. He could not allow her to dissuade him, to snap the thread and leave him dangling from its frayed ends.

"Good day, Lady Blackbourne."

He gave her a brief nod and turned his back, each step he took away from her an agony he would not soon forget.

Chapter Seven

A rran rode back to the house in a daze. The lovely autumn colors surrounding him, the beauty of the ivy where it climbed up the front of the manor house, wasted on him. He sought refuge in his study and stayed there for the better part of the day, burying himself in ledgers and reports and a proposal that had arrived earlier from none other than the new Earl of Blackbourne. It appeared he wished to know more of Arran's plans for expanding into horse breeding, a field Arran excelled at and which he had built upon during his time in Dumfries.

He set the request aside and pushed away from his desk to pour himself a drink. The fire burned low in the hearth and he stoked it well and added another log before taking a seat in front of it. The fire warmed him and cast an amber glow against the brandy in his hand. At his feet, his dog, Fergus, lay curled near the hearth, sleeping contentedly, his long, golden fur burnished rust by the fire.

His meeting with Glory had left him out of sorts.

A gross understatement if ever there was one.

Devastated would be a more apt description. He had

kissed her. It had been a mistake. But the harder he tried to regret it, the more he remembered the feel of her soft lips against his. The sigh of her breath mingling with his own. The curves of her body as he held her in his arms. Even now, more than three decades past, her ability to tantalize him, body and soul, went unabated.

She wanted to try again.

He shook his head. Unreal.

Did she not understand the depth of the hurt she had caused him? Even now, the memory of her betrayal cut into his heart and made it bleed anew. She hadn't even had the courage to tell him herself. Instead, her husband had penned the letter for her, informing him in stark language that she eagerly awaited the arrival of their heir and had no interest in conversing with him further. His repeated attempts to insert himself back into her affections were both foolish and embarrassingly naïve and if they did not stop, his family would pay the price.

Arran wished he could say it was the threat to his family that had stopped him from sending her any further correspondence. It had not been. Rather it was the idea of being a fool, of loving a woman so passionately he had become blind to the fact she no longer returned his feelings. Had she ever? Her rejection had not only broken his heart but also grievously injured his pride. Even now, he could not say which caused the worse pain. A truth that gave him pause and made him wonder—had he justified his wounded ego by claiming it as a broken heart?

If so, he was every bit the fool the late Blackbourne had claimed him to be.

And worse, a coward.

He straightened in his chair, the room suddenly cold around him. Fergus lifted his head at the motion before settling back down with a contented sigh. If only contentedness came so easily to him. But it didn't. Not as he looked back at the choices he had made over the years since and wondered what kind of man he had become. When had he turned his back on the fight and decided it was not worth the effort? How committed had he been that one letter from the great Earl of Blackbourne had been enough to make him turn away? To decide the earl's words echoed Glory's heart and that it was not worth the risk to hear her say so herself?

Because she had always been worth the risk, hadn't she? Once upon a time he had jeopardized everything for her. For them. His family name, his future, his heart. The risk had been for naught. She hadn't loved him enough.

Yet she still wore the locket. Why? Why hang onto an item when you rejected the one who gave it to you? Even her own son claimed she rarely wore any other piece of jewelry with the frequency she did the locket.

Arran leaned back against the cushioned back of the chair and let his gaze crawl up the spines of the books lining the shelves until they reached the exposed beams above.

What did it mean? What was he missing?

"Would it not be worth exploring? Do we not owe each other at least that?"

Was she right? Did they owe each other another chance? And if so, did he possess the courage to try, or was he still a coward, too afraid to risk his heart a second time? He took a deep pull on his drink and closed his eyes, digging deep to find the answers as the brandy warmed a path downward to his heart.

"I am ten times the fool, Lorena. Why, I practically threw myself at him!" Gloria paced her bedchamber, too mortified and heartsick to face her children at dinner, afraid they would see her humiliation, her heartbreak, written into everything she did. Instead, she sent for Lorena, needing to speak to someone she trusted, someone who would not judge her harshly for the things she had done.

"I'm certain it isn't as bad as you believe," Lorena said. "Come sit by the fire and drink some tea."

Gloria fell into the chair near the low-burning fire with a groan and dropped her face into her hands. "It's worse. I kissed him."

Surprise filled Lorena's voice and her tea cup clattered against the saucer. "You did?"

Was that glee she heard? Gloria looked up. Yes. Glee had emblazoned itself all over Lorena's face. For heavens' sake! "Lorena, this is not a happy story! It is the story of the total and utter demise of every last ounce of pride I had left. I didn't simply kiss him. I asked him to kiss me!"

"I see." Lorena leaned forward. "And how was it, this kiss?"

Gloria whimpered and dropped her head into her hands once again. "Glorious."

"Well, I hardly think being on the receiving end of a glorious kiss is anything one should regret. There are not enough glorious kisses in the world, by my estimation. Though one would not know it living in this house. Heavens, I can't turn a corner without finding my daughter and your son locked in an embrace. Or Huntsleigh and Caelie slipping off to heaven knows where. And do not even get me started on Marcus and Rebecca!"

Gloria looked up and blinked at her friend. It was clear she was not taking this situation seriously. "You don't understand.

After the kiss, he turned away from me. He does not share my feelings in the least. How am I to face this man? He is coming to my party in two days hence and, short of rescinding his invitation, I will have no other recourse but to play the happy hostess as if nothing occurred between us!"

"And what did occur between you?"

Had she not been listening? "We kissed!"

"Ah, this time you kissed, but what has transpired before to make you ask for this kiss and for him to turn away after giving it to you? You have told me you knew each other previously, but you have been closed up tighter than Pandora's Box on revealing anything beyond that."

Gloria had rejoiced in Lorena's arrival, thankful to have someone she could confide in. And yet she had kept her silence since then, too afraid of what speaking her secrets aloud would mean. But the burden of them had become too much and, try as she might, she could no longer carry them.

"We were lovers." The words whispered out of her on a breath. A sigh.

"I suspected as much." Lorena laughed lightly. "Don't look so surprised. Roderick and I were lovers first, before we married. Some loves cannot be contained inside the constraints society puts on us with its insistence upon ceremony. Love is love. It keeps its own time and has its own way."

"Well, it had its way with us, that is for certain. Unfortunately, the rest of the world had other plans. My parents had entered into a marriage contract with Blackbourne before my first Season. I begged them to reconsider, but they were more interested in their social standing than in my happiness. And Blackbourne was more interested in winning the jewel of the ton as a bride than in the fact his intended loved another. They allowed me to be presented at court and have my first Season, but my fate was all but sealed."

"And so you had no choice but to break it off with Sir Arran?"

Gloria shook her head. "Perhaps, but I didn't see it then. We made plans to run away. We were going to Gretna Green and then planned to stay in Scotland. Arran had relatives in Dumfries that would take us in. But my parents learned of our plans and they informed Blackbourne. Threats were made, threats to destroy Arran and his family. Blackbourne had the resources to make good on those threats and so I had to choose. I didn't think I could live with myself if I allowed Arran and his family to be destroyed because of me. So I agreed to the marriage and told him good-bye."

The memory of that time, the utter devastation of watching the life she had longed for, was on the cusp of getting, crumble to dust at her feet still had the power to hurt as if it were happening all over again.

She supposed in a way it was.

"And how did he take this news?"

"He was angry. He left and went to London, enlisted in the militia. I wrote him letters begging him to understand but he did not reply."

"Was that the end of it?"

"No." She had thought at the time it was. Despondent, she turned in on herself, numbed her heart and walked through each day an empty shell. Her parents took no notice and Blackbourne cared little. So long as he had what he wanted, that was enough. "Blackbourne procured a special license and we were quickly married. Perhaps he feared if he did not, I might still run. Had Arran returned, likely I would have. But Arran didn't return. Not until it was too late."

Gloria shifted in her chair and stared into the fire. It had been in this room that she last saw him. Blackbourne had insisted they throw a large reception to celebrate their marriage, though in truth their marriage was little more than a sham. Blackbourne had done his husbandly duty the night of their wedding, but had barely touched her since as he spent most of his time in London. She was nothing more than a possession, purchased then set aside and forgotten. He left her behind at Sheridan Park and there she lived in a cage with invisible, yet very real bars. At only seventeen years of age, her life was over. Every dream and hope she'd harbored, set adrift.

"And that was the end of it?"

Gloria hesitated, then shook her head. "Arran's father had passed away and he'd returned to the Sutherland Estates. When he learned of the party, he sneaked in through the kitchens and up to my rooms to await my return. I was over-come, seeing him again. I knew nothing could come of it. I was married, the property of the great Earl of Blackbourne, but in that moment, I cared little for such titles or the vows I had taken. All I wanted was escape. I found that with Arran."

In his arms, the rest of the world disappeared. She was no longer someone else's wife, or a title, or the physical embodi-ment of her parents' expectations. With Arran, she was always just Glory. A woman with a heart and a mind and a body that belonged to her alone.

And that night, she shared it with him, heedless of every-thing and everyone else. Blackbourne and her parents could hang. This was where she belonged. This was who she belonged with, and if she could not have him for an eternity, then she would at least have him that one night.

Even now, she could remember the weight of his body against her own, the warmth of skin on skin and the heat of joining and the passion it culminated in. She committed every moment of that night to memory, fearful it would be their last, and hopeful it was not. The night passed far too quickly and soon dawn came upon them, stealing what little time that remained. Arran slipped away. He had to report back to his unit, but promised he would return. They would find a way, he told her. And, unable to comprehend a life without him, she'd believed.

The following day, Blackbourne left for London. Business, he told her, though she learned later it had been to see his mistress. The same mistress he'd kept for the entirety of their marriage.

"Blackbourne stayed in London for almost two months. During that time, I waited for Arran to return, but he never did."

"And now he has."

She nodded.

"But is that not a good thing?"

"One would think," Gloria sighed. "But things are never as simple or as easy as they look on the surface, I suppose. We have a history of disappointing each other and—" She stopped and shook her head. "Either way. We are ancient history. He has a new life now as heir to the Sutherland Estates and a son to care for. Not to mention his niece, Judith. I suspect there is little room left for me."

Lorena smiled and sat back in her chair. "Then perhaps you need to convince him to make room."

"Easier said than done."

"Nothing ventured, nothing gained," Lorena countered.

But Gloria had traveled that road before and knew the truth. With everything ventured one could still walk away with nothing gained. And everything lost.

"Come," Lorena said, standing from her chair with her hand held out. "Let us leave this melancholy behind. There is a party to plan, is there not?"

Chapter Eight

"I am pleased you have decided to come to the party after all, Uncle."

Arran smiled down at Judith as she straightened his cravat after his incessant tugging at it had set it askew. He did not care for feeling trussed up like a dandy, though both his nieces assured him he could not appear dandified if his life depended on it. He determined this was meant to be a compliment, though Patience seemed less inclined to think so.

"I worried my status as favored uncle might be in jeopardy should I refuse," he said. "Also, your Aunt Beatris would have me drawn and quartered should she return to discover I had not kept good on my promise."

His niece gave a gentle smile and patted his lapel to signify she had finished. "I am sure she would have done nothing of the sort. Though I must admit, had you chosen not to go, I would have been only too happy to stay behind and keep you company."

He shook his head. He worried over Judith's insular nature. She'd had only one Season, sponsored by Beatris, which had proven less than successful with nary a proposal in sight. A fact he found difficult to belief. She was smart, lovely and accomplished. Any man should be lucky to have her as his wife.

Beatris hadn't shared the particulars, but when the time came for a second Season, his niece had refused, causing her father much concern. He'd written to Arran when he'd become ill, worried what would become of his daughter should he not recover, a fact which became more and more likely as his illness progressed. Judith had ignored her father's pleas for her to return to London and instead took up his care, playing nursemaid to him for the last two years of his life.

It had changed her from the light-hearted young woman who had visited him in Dumfries five years earlier. She possessed a depth and a maturity that only harsh reality could create, but along with it came the quiet solitude and acceptance that life did not always work out the way one had imagined it would.

If only his travails had crafted within him the same such acceptance. They hadn't. Decades later, he still wrestled with fate. Fought against it. Wanted to change it.

"If either of you had begged off this party there would be nothing left for Mother to flail her anger upon," Patience announced, sweeping into the room with all the aplomb of a young lady secure in her beauty and the power it wielded. "For I would have done the job for her."

Judith gave a small, indulgent laugh. "Then I guess it is best we prepare to leave, Uncle. For our own safety if nothing else."

Arran joined in his niece's laughter, enjoying the way it lit up her features and showed what a truly beautiful woman she was. Her quiet nature left her at risk of being discounted, overshadowed by her cousin's more deliberate and vivacious beauty. It would be a great loss to any man should he not look a little deeper.

But men were not the most astute or observant of creatures, and young men were the worst culprits of all in this charge.

"Come along then, my beauties," he said, holding out an arm for each to take. "Let us get this ordeal over with, shall we?"

"Uncle," Patience chastised. "I am going to make certain you have the absolute best time this evening, you wait and see. And when we are done, I assure you, you will wish to never leave Sheridan Park ever again."

Arran lifted one eyebrow. "I'm afraid you have set yourself a rather Herculean task, my dear."

Though he recalled clearly one such morning when he awoke to sunlight streaming through the windows and illuminating a certain Countess, giving her ivory skin an ethereal appearance, that he wished just that same thing. To never leave her bedchamber again. To stay with her forever.

"Miss Cosgrove, you are a wonder with a needle and thread," Gloria said, turning this way and that as she stared at the final touches Rebecca's housekeeper had made to a gown a couple years out of fashion. Gloria had finally relented to her daughter's pleas and enlisted Miss Cosgrove's assistance to update a gown purchased before Blackbourne's death. She was more than happy to leave the mourning colors in her past, along with the memories of her marriage. The black had made her appear pasty in her estimation, though the grays had played up the silver shade of her eyes. Regardless, she eagerly returned to the warmer, brighter shades once a year had passed.

"Thank you, my lady." Miss Cosgrove spoke little as she worked. Though pleasant in nature, Gloria had never been able to draw the young woman into any conversation that went beyond mistress and servant. Not that anyone in either household considered her as such. She merely filled the role of housekeeper until Rebecca and Marcus could find a suitable replacement. Though, in Gloria's estimation, they were dragging their feet in that regard. Not that she blamed them. All would sorely miss the young lady's capabilities in running a household, not to mention her ability to transform an ordinary gown into the spectacular concoction that reflected back in the mirror.

Miss Cosgrove gathered her things and left as quietly as she came. Gloria stared at her image in the full length mirror. The gown was a deep claret red with black lace overlay, pulled up in arcs to expose the ruffled hem. The neckline plunged, almost dangerously so, but gave her locket a clear canvas to stand out upon. She did not look even a little like a doddering old widow. She smiled at her reflection and took a deep breath.

Would he notice? Would it change anything if he did?

A soft rap interrupted her thoughts. "Come in." She turned to find Nicholas standing in the doorway, resplendent in the unrelenting black of his evening clothes. Her breath caught. Oh, how much he reminded her of his father in that instant.

"You are even more a vision than usual, Mother. If you keep this up, the younger ladies are going to start refusing to come to our parties for fear of always having to compete for the gentlemen's attentions."

"You are a flatterer of epic proportions, my dear."

"I tell nothing but the truth. Which is just as well, as my wife informs me I am an abominable liar." He smiled and again her heart gave a little twist. His father's smile. "Shall we go? The guests have all arrived and it is time for the guest of honor to make her appearance."

"Everyone has arrived?" More importantly, had Arran

arrived? She feared after their last encounter, she would not see him again. And she must. The time had come for the truth. For explanations. For going beyond their past to a place where they could both find peace.

Nicholas nodded and held out his arm for her. "According to Rebecca and Abigail who, I swear, were mentally checking off names as people swept through the entry way on their way to the ballroom all are present and accounted for. They would not allow me to come for you until they had tallied their lists."

Arran was here.

She took in a calming breath, but it did little to quiet the nerves roiling around in her belly. What if he refused to speak with her? To answer her questions or listen to her explanations? What if he simply turned and walked away after announcing he could go the rest of his life without ever setting eyes upon her and be only too happy?

"Mother?"

She had taken Nicholas's arm but her slippered feet remained rooted to where she stood. She gave a mental shake. *Courage*, her heart whispered. She nodded in answer and forced her legs to move down the sweeping stairwell and long hallway until they reached the closed doors of the ballroom. Nicholas nodded to the footmen. The doors swept open and the music swelled to greet her, full of pomp and circumstance. The crowd parted and Nicholas led her up to stand on the dais occupied by the musicians and their instruments. Once atop it, Gloria's gaze raced through the crowd, searching faces for the one she wished most to see.

Where was he?

The music had stopped and next to her, Nicholas made his speech, but the words drifted past her. Oh, why had they invited so many people? How was she ever to find him amongst the sea of faces filling the ballroom? Panic lifted within her, riddled with the fear he had not come. She needed to speak with him. To set things right. She could not fathom a future without him in it, not now, not that he had finally returned after such a long absence. They deserved this final chance and she was determined to see they had it.

But what if she was the only one who felt that way?

The memory of their kiss invaded her memory and her fear abated. He had kissed her as if no time had passed. As if she were the only woman in the world. As if he loved her still, regardless of how their lives had changed.

Surely that meant something, didn't it?

A rran kept to the outer edge of the crowd as it parted and allowed Glory passage to the dais on the arm of her son. She was a vision, every bit as lovely as the young girl he first met traipsing through the fields on a warm summer's morn. No. Not as lovely. More so. Girlhood had given way to womanhood, and she glided across the floor with a poise and regality that rivaled any queen.

How had he ever thought he deserved a woman such as this? He had been nothing but a boy. The third son of a knighted soldier with no prospects and no skill beyond farming and horses. She had been the daughter of the aristocracy, a shining jewel destined to marry well and live a life of luxury and privilege.

Yet she had loved him. Not only loved him, but been willing to throw away an easy life to make a future with him, at least in the beginning. Could he really blame her for deciding an easy life was better than one filled with struggle or uncertainty?

The question sat uneasy with him. He didn't want to think too hard on it, afraid if he did, his insistence on playing the injured party would begin to crack and peel. If it did, where would that leave him? Would he then have to shoulder some of the blame for the years—decades—they had lost? He did not want such a burden. He had written her repeatedly after their night at Sheridan Park, each letter filled with uncertainty and fear as to why she hadn't responded. When he'd left her in that bed, he had been filled with the confidence of youth that they would find a way to be together. They hadn't, but the blame for that rested on her shoulders, not his.

Didn't it?

The question tormented, worming its way into the crevices doubt created. He tried to shake it off and concentrate on the proceedings.

The new Earl of Blackbourne, who embodied every opposite trait one could imagine when compared to his late father, assisted Glory onto the dais and then turned to speak to the crush of well wishers in front of him. With a confident grin, he began to extol his mother's many virtues.

"Oh, my heavens!" Judith's hand flew to her mouth and her dark, expressive eyes grew wide. She turned to face Arran, and the rest of her words slipped between her fingers. "He looks just like you."

Arran shook his head, rejecting her claim. It made no sense. But as his gaze left his niece and returned to Blackbourne the repeated phrase from others drifted in to haunt him.

You look familiar.

You remind me of someone.

Impossible. His mind rejected the idea outright, but his sight did not lie to him and as he watched the man on the dais —his smile, his gestures—even he reached a point where he could no longer refute the impossibility of it all.

Still, a part of him tried, insisting his eyes deceived. She would have told him! Glory would never have kept such a vital truth from him. His gaze shot to her, to the way her hand rested nervously on the locket he had given her. The locket that housed a lock of her son's hair. Myriad emotions rushed through him with such ferocity he could catch only a hint of them. Anger. Disbelief. Incredulity. Betrayal.

When he'd received the letter from the late Lord Blackbourne, the earl had made a point of informing Arran that the heir to the Blackbourne title was on his way. An arrogant claim, as if he could will the sex of the baby to be as he wished. Arran had not questioned the baby to be Blackbourne's. What man would boast about his wife expecting another man's child, and then pass that child off as the heir to his fortune and title?

Had she duped the late earl as well?

Because seeing Nicholas Sheridan standing next to his mother, the similarities became more and more evident. Not only did he see his own build and coloring and gestures in the man but he recognized several that were also inherent in Callum. The devilish glint of humor in his eyes as if he were up to something, how his smile started in one corner of his mouth, tipping upward before it spread over to the other side.

"Uncle?"

Judith's hand rested on his sleeve. He opened his mouth to tell her it was untrue. That the similarities were nothing more than coincidence, but the words would not come and his niece was far too astute to be fooled by a lie.

"Oh, Uncle." She squeezed his arm and leaned closer. "Should we leave?"

He shook his head and placed a hand over hers. His mind raced and whirled. "No. No, it's fine." What was the point? Leaving would change nothing. He could not un-see what had been seen. He could not un-know it. He could not run from the truth.

The Earl of Blackbourne was his son.

Chapter Nine

The night wore on and despite the well wishes from friends and acquaintances alike, the one person Gloria wished to see most remained elusive. It was as if Arran had turned phantom and disappeared like a wisp of smoke just when she thought she'd caught sight of him. He was here, of that she was certain. Others claimed they had spoken with him, and on several occasions, she had caught sight of Miss Elmsley on the dance floor and once, even Miss Sutherland as she waltzed with Benedict. Their uncle would not have left without them.

And yet, she could find him nowhere, leaving her hope of speaking with Arran, of finally revealing to him the truth about their son and unburdening herself of the secret she had kept all these years, dashed.

A feeling she had more than her share of familiarity with.

The crush of the room pushed against her until she could stand it no longer. She needed to escape, to find a quiet space to regroup, regain her bearings enough to allow her to get through the rest of the party and decide what to do next. It had taken all the strength she had to gather the courage needed to speak to Arran about Nicholas. Would she be able to do it again? Or would fear of his anger and disappointment still her tongue?

She did not know.

Gloria sought out Nicholas and Abigail and found the couple huddled near an alcove half hidden by a large potted plant. "Heavens, you two, there are rooms upstairs." But her admonishment came with a smile, for in truth, she wished everyone felt as free with their affections as her son and daughter-in-law. Such happiness was a beautiful thing to see, and a relief to a mother who'd once feared her son's anger and bitterness would override any chance he had at finding peace and love. She did not want him taking after her in that regard.

Nicholas straightened and cleared his throat. "Mother. Why we were just—uh, that is the, um, plant was looking a little...unwell. I thought to, uh—" He pulled at the plant's leaves and struggled for words.

"Make it jealous?" She suggested.

Her son's cheeks flushed bright red as if he had been caught with his hand in the biscuit jar. "Mother!"

Abigail laughed, enjoying her husband's horrified expression as she swiftly changed the subject. "Are you enjoying your party?"

"I am," Gloria lied. She did not have the heart to tell them otherwise. They had put so much effort into the planning. "But I thought I might step outside and take some air in the garden. Do you think anyone would mind my absence?"

Abigail let go of Nicholas's arm and took Gloria's hands. "Not at all. Are you feeling well?"

"Oh, yes. I am fine. Truly." She forced a smile. "But it is always nice to catch one's breath for the second act, is it not?"

"Of course, Mother." Nicholas leaned down and kissed her cheek. "Shall I escort you?"

"No, no. I will not be long. Stay here and enjoy your...

plant." She smiled and patted Nicholas's cheek as she had when he was a young boy. "I shan't be gone long."

Gloria made her way across the dance floor, stopping periodically to share a few words with revelers. It would not do to appear rude, or as if she were running from her own party, even if that was exactly what she was doing. She needed out. A place to embrace the quiet and sort through her thoughts and what she needed to do next, how to go about it.

She retrieved her shawl and a lantern from the library, then slipped out the French doors and down the steps. The gardens of Sheridan Park were renowned for their vastness and beauty, but to Gloria they were a place of solitude and peace. The mazes and grottos peppered throughout had allowed her an escape during the long years of her marriage. Often she had taken Nicholas with her, to keep him from Blackbourne's sight when he was in one of his rages and looking for someone to slake his anger on. And what better target than the boy—his only heir—who had been fathered by another man.

She searched out her favorite grotto and tucked away inside it, resting the lamp on the stone bench before sitting down. The still night air remained crisp and chilly and she wrapped her shawl tightly about her shoulders to keep from shivering.

Oh, if only she could stay out here for the remainder of the evening. The thought of facing her guests with the heaviness of truth weighing upon her heart offered no enticement to return any time soon. She had spent enough years feigning happiness for the masses, putting a proper face on a properly dismal existence wore one down and she was done with it.

So completely and utterly done.

"It occurred to me this evening—"

Gloria jumped at the unexpected voice and whirled around in her seat, nearly upending the lantern as she came face to face with the man she had spent the better part of the evening searching for.

"Arran!"

The moonlight and lantern conspired to cast sharp shadows against the planes and angles of his face, making him far more handsome than any man had a right to be, if a lady wanted to keep her wits and senses about her. And she did. She had to.

He continued to speak as if she had not, his voice quiet, steady. "—That there is a part of the story that I have missed. A very definitive part. And, for the life of me, I'm not certain how that happened; how it came to be that this particular part of our history was not revealed to me."

He knew.

She tried to breathe, but all the air had rushed out of her lungs, leaving them burning. She attempted to speak, but nothing came, the necessary explanations jumbled and nonsensical and trapped deep within her.

"He is my son." Arran stated the fact plainly, his hand lifting to rest against his chest, near his heart. "Mine. Not Blackbourne's."

He took a step closer and the shadows shifted, illuminating the breadth of his chest and his shoulders where they pressed against the cut of his jacket. His eyebrows dipped and two lines creased between them. So like Nicholas only a few moments before.

Funny, the little things you noticed when your life suddenly teetered on the edge and you knew you were mere seconds from losing your balance and tumbling into a dark abyss.

He laughed, sharp and mirthless. "You know, people kept telling me upon my return that I reminded them of someone, that my face was familiar. I found it odd, given the length of time I had been gone and that I had not known most of these people previous to my departure."

They had seen it too. Even without knowing to look for it, they had seen the similarities just as she had.

She reached out a hand to him; needing to touch him, to anchor herself. "Arran—"

He shook his head. "It wasn't me they were seeing, though, was it? It was your son. *Our* son." The last two words came out harshly, an accusation. She pulled her hand back.

For years, Gloria had lived with the secret, caged into a life of her own making. Not a life she wanted, that was something different all together, but it was the life she'd chosen for reasons that, even now, she did not doubt were sound. And that life, and the secrets it protected, became what she knew, and everything else nothing more than supposition and imagination. A collection of *what ifs*. Scenarios concocted out of *might have beens*. But like most things in life, eventually a time came where one had to answer for their choices.

Her time was now.

"Yes," she whispered past the constriction in her throat. "Yes, Nicholas is your son."

Her voice caught, breaking on the liberty of finally —*finally!*—uttering the words she had wanted to shout from the rooftops for over three decades. She smiled, she could not help herself, for even if every hope she'd dreamed upon Arran's return crumbled to dust at her feet, at least the truth was out. He knew, as he had always deserved to. Blackbourne could not hurt them now. She no longer had to lie and the knowledge of this filled her with an incredible sense of freedom.

"Why did you not tell me?" His fists clenched at his sides and anger emanated from him in waves, beating against her. He looked away as if the sight of her sickened him. Her heart ached. How did she make him understand? He was a proud man. A hero. She knew the thought of being protected would not sit well with him. It never had.

"I did tell you."

His gaze shot back to grab hers. "You lie to me? Still? Do you think I would have forgotten such a conversation as if it bore no significance? He is my son!"

Fury vibrated through him and he stalked as far away from her as the small, enclosed space would allow, one hand diving through his dark hair and leaving furrows. She took a deep breath. He'd always been quick to anger and she bore him no enmity for feeling such vehemence now. But if he knew...if he understood the circumstances, surely...

"Please allow me to explain."

He shook his head and turned back to face her, his hand held out to stave off her words. "There is nothing you can say, Glory. Nothing that can rectify the fact you allowed another man to raise *my* son. Does he even know I am his father?"

"No—"

"Then your lies know no bounds, do they? How easily you have decided who deserved the truth and who received the lies."

"I had no choice! I did what I had to and it was a torture, I assure you!" She vaulted up from the bench and he met her toe to toe.

"Then it was a torture you well-deserved! How dare you keep this from me! You are not the woman I thought you were. I came here this evening thinking I may have behaved in haste to turn you away after our kiss, that perhaps you were right and we did deserve another chance. What a fool I was!"

"You were not a fool." Her voice broke and with it, her heart, torn apart into jagged pieces. "If you will only let me explain. Please, Arran!"

She extended a hand toward him again, but he brushed her away and took a step back beyond her reach. "We are over," he whispered in the same steady, quiet voice he had first used upon entering the grotto. It echoed with finality and promised no absolution or understanding. "Whatever chance may have existed for us has been forever extinguished by your lies and secrets."

Arran turned on his heel like a soldier executing a swift maneuver and marched out of the grotto. Out of her life.

Her knees gave way and she sank to the cold ground, its hardness offering no reprieve from the pain echoing through her. A sob caught in her throat and then broke free, bringing with it a torrent of all the pain she had suffered, all the guilt she had carried, all the hopes she had lost.

"Mother?"

How long had she cried before Nicholas found her? It hardly mattered. She looked up into his handsome face, the whisper of his father living and breathing through him. For the longest time, seeing this had given her the strength she'd needed to keep going. Now, its existence only mocked her, another dagger through her broken heart.

She wiped at the tears where they stained her cheeks. Her eyes burned but her conscience demanded she was not yet done.

Nicholas assisted her to her feet. "What is it? Are you injured? Did someone—"

She shook her head. "No. This is my own doing."

He gave her a confused look. "Your own doing? I don't understand."

"I know." She waved a shaking hand toward the stone bench where the lantern still burned. "Sit down, my sweet boy. There is something I must tell you."

Chapter Ten

"You, sir, are an idiot and a coward."

If Arran thought this horrid night was at an end, he was sadly mistaken. After his confrontation with Glory, a battle that left no true victor, he had collected his nieces and returned home, his anger a tangible entity shadowing his every move. Upon arriving, he sought out the sanctuary of his study and a bottle of brandy to numb his heart, but the fine liquor offered no solace or oblivion.

"Forgive me, Sir," the butler squeaked from behind the irate man filling the doorway. "I told him you were not in but—"

Arran stood and faced the Earl of Blackbourne. His son. "Leave us, Edger. It is fine."

The butler quickly acquiesced and the doors closed behind Nicholas's imposing figure, caging his anger inside the four walls of the study.

"How dare you," the younger man seethed. The hands fisted at his sides shook, his need to do violence palpable. That he didn't was a testament to his character and somehow, in some odd way, it made Arran proud. In his younger years, he had not controlled his temper so well. He'd been quick to anger and quicker to act, yet far too slow to regret and apologize.

He often wondered if he hadn't left for London when Glory first made her decision to marry Blackbourne, if he had stayed and tried to convince her to change her mind, would the outcome have been different?

The question haunted him now, but for far different reasons.

"And what is it I have dared?" He stepped away from the warmth of the fire and set the snifter of brandy on his desk.

They were of a height and build. And while his unannounced guest had an even paler version of his mother's silvery eyes, it was his elder brother's straight nose and Arran's firm mouth and sharp cheekbones that had been cobbled together to create the rest of his handsome visage. How strange to see such similarities in someone you had only just met. Stranger yet that others had noticed it before he, even if they lacked the ability to put the full story together.

"Mother has told me the truth."

"Ah." Arran nodded. "How noble of her. Yet, you do not seem anywhere near as angry as I over it. Why is that?"

"Because I was not so oblivious to the truth as you." He spoke the fact like an accusation, like somehow Arran should have known. Should he? The question poked at his conscience, but Nicholas pressed on before he could explore the sensation further. "I have known since I was a boy that Blackbourne was not my true father. He made certain of that, and even more certain that I knew the moment another male heir was borne, I would be sent away, as would my mother."

"Then you have known for some time. A luxury I was not afforded."

"That Blackbourne was not my father, yes. That it was you, no. That I learned tonight."

"And yet you show up on my doorstep and accuse me of being an idiot and...what was the other thing?"

One of Nicholas's dark eyebrows arched upward. "A coward."

"Hm. I cannot claim I have never been called an idiot before, however, a coward—I fail to see the correlation between the two in conjunction with this particular issue. Perhaps you could enlighten me?"

"You are a coward, *sir*, because you ran off into the night instead of staying and fighting for something that is far more precious than your damnable pride." Nicholas spat out the last word as if it left a bad taste in his mouth. As if he had drunk the same elixir, only to discover it contained nothing but poison.

"I left," he countered. "Because your mother has lied to me for over thirty years. Because she has kept you from me all this time, disallowed me the opportunity to be a father to you, a husband to her—"

"She had a husband!" Nicholas's shout echoed against the walls, soaked into the bookcases, rattled the windows. "Or did you forget that when you laid with her the night of my conception?"

His accusation set Arran aback, unprepared for it as he was. He had built his defense based on Glory's culpability. She had done this. She had not done that. He had not excised his own accountability. But Nicholas had the right of it. Arran had sneaked into her room that night, into her bed. His only thought had been in claiming her, proving his love was the one she needed, deserved. Proving her wrong in her decision to marry Blackbourne.

A truth conveniently disregarded over the years when the pain of losing her made it easier to forget. Blaming her, venting his anger on her memory and betrayal, had kept him going. Kept him from falling apart.

But his son's pointed accusation no longer afforded him such ignorance.

Nicholas took a step closer. "I sometimes wondered who you would be. I invented every kind of scenario and every reason imaginable as to why my mother broke her marriage vows to be with you. But one part of it remained clear to me—whatever it was, it had left her broken-hearted. She mourned your loss every day of my life. She mourns it still."

Nicholas's words cut into him, slicing with sharp blades until he was left scrambling to pull together some semblance of a defense on his behalf. "She made her decision."

Nicholas closed the space between them until they stood nose to nose. His son possessed a very formidable presence. "What would you have had her do differently? Should she have abandoned her husband and son? Blackbourne had claimed me as his own for the sake of his pride, to not appear the cuckold, but he resented every moment of it and he let us both know at every opportunity. Mother protected me as best she could from his rages, but it meant she took the brunt of it. And Blackbourne made it clear, if she did not play the part of his wife as he expected, if she tried to leave, he would destroy her, me—and you."

Arran's heart stilled. "What are you talking about?"

"I did not know who you were. Your name was never to be spoken in our home, your very existence ignored. But I still remember the threats. Blackbourne's promises to destroy you and your family should she not hold up her end of the agreement."

Back then, Arran's father had borrowed money from Blackbourne to expand the estate's resources. If Blackbourne wanted, he could have called in those debts. They could have lost everything. But Douglas Sutherland was not a man who took defeat sitting down. "My family would have survived regardless of what he tried to do. She could have left him."

Nicholas barked out a laugh and shook his head, giving Arran a look that clearly imparted what an idiot he thought he was. It rankled. "If my mother had left Blackbourne, she would have had to leave me behind with a man who hated and resented my very existence. Would that have been a more palatable solution for you? Do you think she would have lived happily ever after knowing she had forfeited her son for her own desires? That she had left me in harm's way?"

Arran turned away from Nicholas's question, but the words battered against his back. Sickened him. Refused to be ignored. He turned and sank into one of the chairs facing the fire as the truth blasted through him like a cannonball, taking chunks out of the resentment and anger and leaving behind a landscape he did not recognize.

Had he not been so hurt and angry, would he have seen the truth of it? And if he had, would it have changed things? Would he have seen the wisdom of her decision and agreed it would be for the best? That ruining the lives of others so they could have what they wanted would never bring them the happiness they sought. Or would his pride and anger have made him behave recklessly, risking their futures and that of their son?

He had no answer. Or rather he did, but could not yet give it voice. Because in doing so it robbed him of his ability to beat his chest and brand himself the victim. But were his injuries any more severe than hers? Had he not gone on with his life? Married and had a son while she had been consigned to a marriage that amounted to little more than a prison sentence. What had her life been like, living every day, knowing what she did, and what he didn't?

For a time, he'd wished that she lived each day with the misery of her mistake, that she suffered as he did. Guilt stabbed at him. She had not made a mistake at all. She had made a sacrifice. She had offered herself up so that his life would be untouched by Blackbourne's wrath. So that their son and Arran's family would not be destroyed in the fallout.

Glory had more bravery than any soldier he'd stood next to on the battlefield, and not once had she faltered in her cause. Not once had she asked for his help, knowing if he offered it Blackbourne would have destroyed everyone she held dear.

But what had it cost her?

"Did she know no happiness at all?"

Nicholas sighed. For a moment, Arran watched a flicker of guilt cross his features and realized even without knowing the full story, their son had been aware of the sacrifice she'd made for him. That she had protected him as best she could and given him a better life than he would have had if she had left her husband to run off with another man.

"She had moments, with Rebecca and me. Times when Blackbourne was away and she could let down her guard. But it took its toll." He shook his head and his voice softened. "When he died, all I could think of was, thank God she's free of him now. I have never known a woman of such strength and determination. At least not until I met my wife."

"I did not know." But how hard had he tried? He had been so wrapped up in his own bitterness, he'd turned a blind eye to everything else. He refused to entertain any idea that didn't paint her in the role of villain and he, the victim. It was easier that way. It gave his hurt and anger a place to go.

But he hadn't been the true victim at all. He had been able to walk away, while she and Nicholas had been left behind with a man who hated Glory for her betrayal and resented Nicholas for being born. What had he endured that came close to that?

The realization crawled over him like a sickness, peeling away the years and rebuilding them in a new light. He wrapped his arms around his middle as if he could contain it or hold it at bay. He could not.

Glory had stayed with Blackbourne to protect her son.

Their son.

A slow breath eased out of him, the anger and bitterness seeping away with it, leaving plenty of room for self-incrimination and harsh reality. He had treated her abominably, knowing what he did now. How would she ever forgive him his harsh words? Likely she would not. She had offered him an olive branch, a second chance, and he had batted it away like a petulant child. If she refused to speak to him again, it was nothing less than he deserved.

He waved a hand toward the other chair. "Sit. Please. I have a feeling there is much more for us to discuss."

His son hesitated. He did not blame him. But after a moment, he issued a grave nod and father and son talked well into the night.

"You have been an absolute bear, brother dear. I wonder if perhaps we should not send you off to hibernate until this pique you are in ends." Beatris sipped from the tea delivered upon her arrival in the sitting room. She had returned home earlier in the day, her meeting with the Duke and Duchess Franklyn not going quite as well as she had planned. It appeared her son was less enamored of the Duke's daughter than Beatris had hoped and she'd left her husband behind in the city for the purpose of changing their son's mind.

Arran had purposely chosen the sitting room for his breakfast as he'd thought his sister would not think to look for him here. Unfortunately, it appeared his older sibling had a sixth sense when it came to his whereabouts.

"If my mood is so unbearable, perhaps you should find somewhere else to drink your tea," Arran stated, staring out the window. Dark clouds approached from the north, promising an autumn storm was on its way. He welcomed it, a clear reflection of his mood these past two days as he wrestled with what he knew, what he had done.

How close he'd stood to a second chance with Glory. And how quickly he had allowed his pride and anger to destroy it.

"Nonsense. How am I ever to get to the bottom of what has you in such a state if I do not sit here and interrogate you mercilessly?"

He closed his eyes and leaned his forehead against the cool glass. "Oh, please don't."

He heard the smile in her tone when she answered. "Now, you know better than that, Arran. I simply lack the ability to walk away and leave my baby brother in turmoil."

"I am not a baby."

"Then perhaps you could stop sulking like one and tell me what is wrong."

She would not leave. And if he tried to, she would follow, dogging his every step until he finally relented. He let out a long, slow breath. What did it matter? Perhaps the scandal of his fathering a son with a married woman would horrify her to such a degree she would let the matter drop and never mention it again.

"I have received news that has distressed me."

"About the Earl of Blackbourne?"

Arran spun around on his heel and faced his sister, his eyes wide. Did she possess the sight? He'd heard stories of relatives from generations past who had made such claims. He had always pushed it aside as pure balderdash, but—

"Oh heavens, Arran, don't look so shocked. Judith was most worried and I wormed what information I could out of her."

"Then you know he is my son?"

"I do." She gave a wry smile. "Quite a pickle, I will admit, and likely a good thing Father is long since dead and buried as I'm sure he would have a pretty word or two to say on the matter."

Arran made a face. Falling in love with Glory had displeased his father greatly, but Arran, possessing all the brashness of youth, ignored him, selfishly wanting what he wanted and not looking beyond the ramifications his actions would cause.

Unlike Glory.

"I made a horrible mistake, blaming her for everything that happened between us," he admitted, saying the words aloud for the first time. "She tried to explain but I..."

He stopped and shook his head, his shoulders drooping in defeat.

"You likely railed at her and then stormed off."

He clenched his teeth, the back molars grinding against each other. His sister knew him too well. "Perhaps."

"Hm. Well, tell me this then," Beatris said, stopping long enough to take another sip of tea. "When Callum makes a mistake, what counsel do you give him to rectify the situation?"

"I tell him to apologize to the injured party and make amends."

"Well, there you have it. Your own words have given you a solution to your problem."

"I have made grievous errors. Said things I cannot retract. Caused her much hurt."

Beatris set her cup and saucer on the silver tea tray and stood, walking over to him to take his hands in hers. "My dear brother. You need to stop seeing everything as only black or white. Life exists in all different shades. Go. Talk to her. Listen to what she has to say and then go from there. If you do not at least do that, you will regret it for the rest of your life."

"I can't imagine there is much room left inside of me for regret."

"Oh, sweetheart—" She patted his cheek and smiled. "There is always room for more regret."

He feared Beatris was right. Outside, the dark clouds rumbled and made good on their promise as the first raindrops splattered against the window behind him.

Chapter Eleven

T he next two days dragged by, the unrelenting minutes growing slower with each swing of the pendulum in the old clock atop the mantle of the solar. Gloria had sent Abigail to bed over an hour earlier. Her daughter-in-law's well-intended hovering had exhausted her and yet she remained restless and unable to sleep. Her family meant well and she loved them for it, but her heart wanted nothing more than to surround itself in silence and lick its grievous wounds. Now that the last of the party guests who had stayed at Sheridan Park had departed for their own homes ahead of the rain, she could do just that.

Arran was lost to her forever. The revelation of a lifetime of secrets had made that fact painfully clear.

She rose from the chaise and walked to the window, staring out into the night. Rainclouds smothered the moon and stars, turning the night inky black and pelting the earth with their fury.

With a sigh, she turned from the darkness and rain and left the solar to find the solace of her bedchamber. Perhaps she could pull the covers over her head and sleep until the worst of the pain abated. How long would it take? A week? A month? A lifetime?

She gave a sad smile as she passed through her bedroom door and closed it behind her. Time had a strange kind of irrelevancy now. She had told her truth. Those who needed to know did. There was nothing else she could do.

Perhaps that was the worst of it. She could not fix it. She could not undo the pain she had caused. Or take back the secrets she had kept. Nor could she claim she would have done anything differently upon discovering she carried Arran's child.

The carved wood of her oak door pressed into her back as she leaned against it. A fire burned low in the hearth, chasing out the damp and replacing it with a comforting warmth. She breathed in the scent of it. In a moment, she would need to call for Doreen to assist her in undressing, but not yet. She opened her eyes and pushed away from the door to sit near the fire. Perhaps the flames would penetrate the cold that had invaded her bones.

Before she reached the chair, a shadow flickered at the corner of her vision, out of place within the stillness of the room. She whirled about to face it, her heart instantly in her throat as a figure approached, the darkness slipping away from him like water off a duck's back. Unlike a duck, however, this intruder was quite drenched.

"How did you get in here?"

Arran stepped closer, stopping at the corner of her bed. He had removed his coat, but his buckskin breeches bore stains from the rain and his hair was damp and in disarray.

A host of memories rushed forth from the last time they occupied this space, bringing with them a longing she could not contain or control. "The same way I did over thirty years ago. I sneaked in. With a little assistance this time from your daughter and her husband, I might add."

Hope soared within her breast, but her injured heart held it fast, kept it tethered. She had learned her lesson in that regard. Likely he wanted nothing more than to hear the rest of the story. Or to berate her for the parts he already knew. She gripped her hands together and pressed into her abdomen, braced for whatever was to come.

He approached her, an apparition pieced together from memory and heartbreak. He stopped in front of her and reached out a hand to lift the locket at her breast. As he had only days ago—was it really only days?—he pressed his thumb against the clasp and with slow, deliberate movements, lifted the top. His thumb gently brushed the lock of Nicholas's hair curled within.

"I spoke to our son," he whispered.

Her gaze lifted swiftly to his, but his expression gave nothing away. "When?"

"He came to visit me the night of the party."

"I did not know. He said nothing to me."

The corner of Arran's mouth lifted slightly as he continued to stare at the inky black curl. "Ah, well, he said plenty to me. It seems he was quite displeased with my behavior toward you and decided I needed to be educated on all the things I did not know."

Her heart pounded against her ribs. "What did he say?"

"He told me of Blackbourne's threats to destroy my family and our son. I had no idea." He closed the locket and looked up at her then and for the first time the hardness of his gaze softened. "And he called me a coward."

"You are not a coward."

"On the contrary. I abandoned you. Your rejection of me in favor of Blackbourne injured my pride and bruised my ego and so I turned tail and ran. I blamed you for everything, just as I did the other night. When I first learned you were with child, a part of me wondered...feared it might be mine. I sent letters, but—"

"You did?"

"Yes, of course."

She shook her head. "Blackbourne must have intercepted them before they reached me."

"Which explains why it was he who responded to them, telling me you were happy with your new position and that the babe belonged to him."

She took in a swift breath and pain twisted in her chest. How it must have felt to receive such a letter! "I had no idea he had done such a thing. I had no part in it, I swear to you."

He nodded. "I realize that now. But at the time, I was ready to swoop in to rescue you like some knight in shining armor. Instead, I allowed his words to harden my heart against you. Dammit, Glory! I should have known better! I should have come for you."

Gloria reached up and placed a hand over Arran's where he continued to grip the locket. "There was nothing you could have done. Nothing either of us could have done. In the eyes of the law, I was Blackbourne's property. He had claimed Nicholas as his own to save his reputation and pride. If I had tried to leave him—"

"He would have kept the boy."

"Yes. I couldn't leave Nicholas to him. Blackbourne was a heartless man. He resented our son and as the years went on and I did not give birth to another son of his blood, his resentment turned to loathing. He needed Nicholas or the title and lands would pass to a distant cousin he despised. He would not have it. But it did not stop him from treating our son like an interloper. In the end, he left Nicholas nothing more than the title and entailed properties. The rest went to Rebecca." She shook her head, the memories painful even now. "I did the best I could to protect him, but it was never enough."

"He told me what you did. What you endured. If I had known, I would have come for you regardless. Why did you not send for me?"

"I did. I wrote you when I discovered I carried our child. I begged you to come, to save me. Save us."

He shook his head. "A letter I never received. Shall I assume he intercepted yours as well?"

She nodded. "Yes, although I did not discover this until years later. At the time, I assumed you wanted nothing to do with us."

"I wanted everything to do with you." Closing the locket, he let it go and cupped her face, his hands calloused and cold. His touch set off a fire deep in her belly. "God help me, I still do. The moment I saw you again, I knew I could no longer deny it. Your absence has haunted me since the moment I left that bed behind us and it has tormented me every day since. But your son—*our son*—was correct. I have been a coward. And a fool. I let pride shut my eyes to what you suffered so I might wallow in my own hurt and bitterness. I locked my heart away and refused to listen when the sight of you, your very nearness, made it whisper once again. I turned away. Again and again."

His words cut the tethers and the hope in her heart lifted, set free. "But you are here now, as am I. That is enough."

He looked at her, into her, and awakened every sensation he had ever evoked within her. "You are far too forgiving."

"I am far too cognoscente of the passing of time. We have lost three decades. I do not wish to lose another day, do you?"

"I do not." He smiled and it stirred a commotion inside of her that refused to be tamped down. How she wanted this man. Had always wanted him. Dreamed of this moment without ever believing it could truly happen. And now here he was, standing in her bedchamber, his hand touching her skin, his lips but a breath away.

"What shall you do about it then?"

"I suppose I could court you. We never did have a proper courtship."

She gave a light laugh. "No, we did not." They had spent their days meeting in secret, loving in shadows. It had been exciting, courting scandal in such a way. "And what would you consider a proper courtship?"

His hand spread the breadth of her cheek and his mouth touched the arch of her cheekbone where he placed a soft kiss. Her eyes fluttered closed. "This, perhaps? Is that proper?"

"It feels properly wonderful."

She felt the curve of his smile upon her skin. His arms slipped around her as his mouth moved to her neck, trailing a line of heat downward until it met her collarbone. "And this?"

"Oh, yes. Very proper indeed."

"Hm." His hands moved behind her and pulled at the laces of her dress until the material loosened around her. "This?"

"This may be bordering on improper. Sinful, even."

"I see. Should I stop?"

She caught his gaze, the mischief she saw there taking her back as if no time had passed at all. "You most definitely should not."

"I do not wish to compromise you."

"I would very much like you to compromise me. In fact," she said, growing bold as she undid the buttons of his waistcoat and pushed the damp wool down off his shoulders. "I would very much like you to compromise me in as many ways possible."

He straightened his arms and let the waistcoat drop to the floor. "How very scandalous."

She lifted her eyebrows and sought his mouth, no longer able to hold back the torrent of emotion and need building inside of her. She kissed him, fully, deeply, finally allowing everything she had held in heart pour out and into him. And he returned it, exploring her with his own kiss, his hands pulling at his cravat and tossing it aside, then tugging his shirt from his breeches and over his head until it fell somewhere behind him, freeing him to rescue her from her dress.

When he spoke, his words came on heavy breaths. "I'm afraid, my lady, that I have a very urgent need to be very, very improper and wondered if you might join me on that very large bed looming behind us."

"I think I would be quite amenable to that, sir."

"Wonderful. Also, I'm curious as to your ability to liberate me from these boots. It will make getting the rest of my clothing off much easier."

She laughed as her dress slipped over her hips and pooled at her feet. Oh, how wonderful the laughter felt. How long it had been kept caged. But no more.

"I believe my valet skills are a bit rusty, but I will do my best."

And she did, the two of them giggling like untried youths, fumbling about until the boots were removed and his wet breeches peeled from his skin, revealing the muscular length of his legs and the outline of his erection through his under-clothes.

He quickly turned her about and undid the laces of her stays, removing the last bit of both their clothing before he swept her up in his arms and placed her gently onto the down mattress and covered her with his heat.

"My God," he whispered as skin touched skin. "How I have dreamed of this."

"As have I." She had envisioned this for so long it was diffi-cult to believe it was not simply another figment of her imagi-nation. She lifted a hand, touching his chest and feeling the steady beat of his heart beneath her palm. He was real. *This* was real.

Arran lifted above her and let his gaze roam over her nakedness. "I had almost forgotten how amazingly beautiful you are."

She shook her head. "I am over thirty years older and have given birth to two babies." "A fact that only adds to your beauty. You're an angel that has fallen to earth."

"Then will you take me to heaven, my love?"

He chuckled. "I shall certainly try."

She pulled him back to her and they collapsed together into the soft down, their bodies sighing with pleasure.

"The memory of how wonderful you feel against me pales in comparison to the reality," he said and tightened his arms around her. She wrapped her legs around his hips, cradling him so that his hardness pressed into her, taunting her, thrilling her. Before, their lovemaking had been rushed, furtive and yet somehow wonderful. But tonight, she planned on taking her time, relishing each moment, cherishing every sensation. Over and over again.

Arran's mouth left hers and burned a trail down her throat, her chest, and then captured her nipple to savor the taste of her as she threaded her hand into his hair, wanting to hold him there forever and yet pull him away, afraid she would lose her mind to the pleasure he gave.

"Arran. I thought we might take it slow, but I think I have changed my mind. I have waited long enough." Her whole body ached for him and demanded release.

"You have no idea how happy I am to hear you say that." He shifted slightly and the tip of his shaft eased into her, hard and full. She sighed and a low moan escaped her as he pushed in further, filling her completely.

He stopped and rested his forehead against hers.

"Arran?"

"Ssh. I'm savoring the moment."

She laughed and wiggled until his breath caught in his throat. "Which moment is that?"

"The one where I finally found my way back home."

Tears moistened her eyes and she leaned up on her elbows to kiss him, to tell him with her touch that he was home to her as well, and she had no intention of allowing either of them to wander off again. But the kiss only made the ache increase and soon, they let their bodies do the talking, rocking against each other until words gave way to sensation and sighs and moans of exquisite pleasure. It crested within her, wrapped around her and carried her over the edge with him and in that moment she knew.

He was hers. Finally. Completely. Forever.

"I love you, my shining knight. Always." She kissed him and in the depth of it knew their love had never abated, that it had always lived beneath everything they did, waiting, knowing. They only had to find a way to forgive and understand to resurrect it and set it free.

A rran awoke slowly with the realization that something was different. As his body caught up with his mind, and the warmth of another body seeped into his, warming some parts, heating others to an almost painful degree, the previous night filtered back.

Glory. He smiled and opened his eyes and squinted. Sunlight rushed in through the opening in the curtains and fell against the bed in a wide golden swath, illuminating the angel who slept in his arms.

It hadn't been a dream.

She shifted as if sensing his attention and opened her eyes to stare up at him with her beautiful silver eyes. Her long, blonde curls cascaded across the pillow beneath her and down over her shoulders to rest upon her exposed breast. Unable to help himself, he bent and kissed her there, his groin stirring in response.

"Good morning, my love."

She stretched and turned, pushing her hips against his burgeoning erection, a sinful smile lighting her beautiful features. He threaded his fingers through her hair and kissed her, softly, sweetly, before pulling away to stare at her once again. He would never tire of the view of her. For years to come, he would gaze upon her face and remember this moment when his future settled around him and with it the certainty that it would stretch into eternity.

"Promise me we shall not allow another day to pass where we will be apart. I'm not sure I could bear it," he said.

"How shall we manage such? Shall we take turns sneaking back and forth to each other's homes?" Her eyes sparked and her smile broadened.

"If I didn't know better, I would think you relish the clandestine nature of such a suggestion. But I had something else in mind."

"And what did you have in mind?" Glory slipped her hand around his waist, but it inched downward to his buttock and gave a gentle squeeze. Desire rushed through him and he struggled to keep his mind on the task at hand despite his body's demands that he attended to its needs first.

"Something of a more permanent nature, perhaps."

"Permanent? That sounds quite conventional."

"I'm a conventional man. And I have waited a lifetime to finally call you mine."

She stretched her body up to place a kiss against his lips and the thin thread that kept him from taking her frayed a little more. "I have always been yours, Arran. Every day since the first day I met you. Not once did my heart falter in my feelings for you. Not for a moment."

"Nor did mine. No matter how hard I tried to bury them

under my hurt and anger. But over thirty years ago, I promised I would marry you and I mean to make good on that promise if you will let me."

"Mm." She smiled against his lips as she kissed him once more, setting fire to the thread that tethered his sanity. "I must admit I much prefer the title of Mrs. Sutherland over the Dowager Countess of Blackbourne. And if, in return, I get to spend my days and nights with you, it is not even a question I need to think about. I will marry you, Sir Arran Sutherland, and I will spend the rest of our lives making up for the years we have been apart. In fact, I would be most appreciative if we could start now."

Her hand moved between them and gripped his hardness. A low groan escaped him. "Good Lord, woman. If you keep this up, I will have no other choice but to rush you to the altar immediately."

He rolled on top of her, relishing her laughter, free and lovely as it had once been long ago. The sound was a balm to his wounded heart, filling the empty crevices and healing the scars. He held her close and breathed her in. She smelled of fresh daisies on an early summer morning. She felt like peace.

"I love you," he said. "Always and forever."

"Which is what we have now, my love." She touched his face and looked deep into his eyes until her gaze reached all through him. "Always and forever."

A Sneak Peek

∽⁓つ

BOOK 5: SURRENDER TO SCANDAL

"Have you heard a word I've said, Glenmor?"

Benedict Laytham pulled his attention away from the window and returned it to Marcus Bowen, who had come by to discuss several investments they'd made and future ones he had in mind. The man's brain never sat idle.

"Forgive me, I had just..." He let his words trail off. He had just what? Been staring like a lovesick schoolboy at the carriage conveying Miss Judith Sutherland up the drive to Sheridan Park? Hardly respectable behavior for the Earl of Glenmor, now was it? He cleared his throat and straightened. "Never mind. You were saying?"

He'd had a devil of a time concentrating on Marcus's report. A most disconcerting situation, given the current state of the Glenmor finances. But the fact was, he had not been expecting Miss Sutherland to stop by this afternoon and her sudden presence had left him with an unwanted sense of disquiet. He really needed to get over this. It was inevitable that he would run into her with relative frequency, given he was staying at Sheridan Park while the Glenmor countryseat,

Maple Glen Manor, underwent much-needed—and frighteningly costly—repairs. According to his sister, Abigail, Miss Sutherland was assisting with the wedding planning for her uncle to the Dowager Countess of Blackbourne, indicating the young woman had a most orderly mind.

Still, he wished he'd had enough notice prior to the lady's arrival to remove himself from the premises. Taken a long walk and avoided the temptation of her.

"I said our return on investment in Booth's Liverpool and Manchester Railway will prove most lucrative over time and should help immensely with rebuilding the Glenmor coffers." Marcus, never one to mince words where business matters were concerned, crossed the room to stand at the window and peer outside. "What are you looking at? I swear your mind is elsewhere today."

Benedict turned away from the window to face the interior of the room. "Nothing in particular."

He tried to shake off the idea of Miss Sutherland, of the fact that she was only at the other end of the long hallway. If he kept this up, Marcus would no doubt figure out what had him so addle-brained. The man had an acute sense of observation that could be unnerving at times.

Miss Sutherland had proven to have the oddest effect on Benedict. Disturbing, really, and for the life of him, he could not pinpoint exactly why. She was not beautiful, at least not in the conventional sense. She dressed plainly and kept to a rather sedate palate of colors. In fact, she still wore her mourning garb of dark grays and pale mauves, though over six months had passed since her father had died. Nor did she arrange her thick, chestnut brown hair in an attractive coif. Instead, she pulled it back into a tidy bun at the nape of her slender neck. She did not wear baubles or such fripperies that most ladies of his acquaintance seemed to prefer. She did none of the usual things that brought one's attention to a lady, and yet...

He sighed. Yet she possessed the most expressive eyes he had ever seen. Deep and dark and steeped in mystery, as if she hid a secret she did not wish to tell.

Which was ridiculous. She'd spent the past two years playing nursemaid to her dying father. Before that, she'd had but one Season in London that, according to his sister, had been most uneventful. What possible secrets could she have locked away so tightly?

Marcus glanced out the window one last time, then back at Benedict, arching one dark eyebrow upward as if reading his thoughts. Most disconcerting.

Benedict left the window and crossed the room to his desk —or rather Blackbourne's desk that he had borrowed for his visit—and picked up the papers Marcus had brought with him. The numbers were indeed favorable and he breathed a small sigh of relief. The improvements to Maple Glen's manor house were costing more than he had intended, but the work was necessary.

Attracting a wealthy bride to help alleviate the chokehold on the family finances had proven far more difficult than he'd expected. Apparently, the title of Countess to an impoverished and scandal-ridden title was not considered a fair exchange. A true pity, as without a bride in possession of an ample dowry, he had little hope of refilling the Glenmor coffers his uncle had decimated before his untimely death.

Also by Kelly Boyce

THE SINS & SCANDALS SERIES

Book 1: An Invitation to Scandal

Book 2: A Scandalous Passion

Book 3: A Sinful Temptation

Book 4: The Lady's Sinful Secret

Book 5: Surrender to Scandal

Book 6: A Sinner No More

Book 7: The Sweetest Sin

Book 8: A Most Scandalous Christmas

Book 9: A Hint of Scandal

THE BRIDES OF FATAL BLUFF

Book 1: The Outlaw Bride

SALVATION FALLS

Book 1: Salvation in the Rancher's Arms

Dear Reader

Thanks so much for reading **THE LADY'S SINFUL SECRET** – I have been wanting to tell this secret since writing the first book and leaving the unanswered question of Nicholas's father and how that all came about. I had a few ideas, but I never dreamed once I started writing the story I would discover a whole new family with cast of characters who demanded their own stories.

The Sutherlands are a wonderful group of characters you be seeing more of, beginning with the next book in the series, **SURRENDER TO SCANDAL.** The very handsome Earl of Glenmor, Benedict Laytham is in need of a wealthy bride, unfortunately a pesky thing called love keeps getting in his way when he meets Miss Judith Sutherland.

For those of you who were introduced to the series with this novella, find out where it all began with AN INVITATION TO SCANDAL (Nicholas & Abigail) and what came after with, A SCANDALOUS PASSION (Spencer & Caelie) and A SINFUL TEMPTATION (Marcus & Rebecca).

To keep up to date on what's new, upcoming releases, a sneak peeks on cover reveals and be entered into contests, please visit my website at www.kellyboyce.com and sign up for my newsletter.

If you enjoyed this book, please consider leaving an honest review at your favorite retailer. It is always appreciated!

All the best ~ *Kelly*

Acknowledgments

When I sit down to write the acknowledgements for my books, I realize I have the same people to thank each time. This is the great benefit of having such wonderful friends and family who continue to support and encourage me on this crazy ride.

So for my family – thank you once again for creating such a solid foundation and instilling a strong work ethic and, perhaps most importantly, crazy sense of humor. Without these things, I likely wouldn't be typing this now.

To my best friend, Lisa MacDougall for all those writing sessions after school and through the weekend that fuelled my love of the written word and made it impossible for me to dream of being anything else.

For my writing posse who answer my questions, share my frustrations and remind me all this is doable no matter how hard it gets: Pamela Callow, Julianne MacLean, Cathryn Fox, Anne MacFarlane and Annette Gallant. You ladies rock.

Nancy Cassidy – my wonderfully patient editor, thanks for making me look good.

And last but never least – my awesome husband, John. You changed my life, too.

About the Author

Kelly Boyce started writing stories in Grade 2 when her favorite teacher, Mrs. Matheson, showed up with a box filled with plot ideas and she was immediately hooked. But it wasn't until she read Lisa Gregory's *Bitterleaf* that she fell in love with historical romance. Once she discovered Romance Writers of Atlantic Canada and learned how to turn those stories into books, it was full steam ahead.

A life-long Nova Scotian, Kelly lives near the Atlantic Ocean with her amazing husband and a clownish golden retriever with a stubborn streak a mile wide. She loves writing stories about relationships and creating a sense of community around the hero and heroine filled with secondary characters who take on a life of their own.

Along with *The Sins & Scandals Series*, she has also released several western historical romances with Harlequin. The first two, **The Outlaw Bride** and **Salvation in the Rancher's Arms** will soon be re-released under her own banner, while the remaining, **Salvation in the Sheriff's Arms**, and two Christmas novellas: **The Cowboy of Christmas Past** and **Christmas in Salvation Falls** are still available through Harlequin.

Currently, she is hard at work developing a new three book series on the Lindwell Family, who were introduced in *The Sins & Scandals Series*.

Copyright